Betrayal
at the
Opera

Betrayal at the Opera

LINDA A. MORTON

ISBN# 979-8-218-85282-5

Interior design and formatting by:

E.M.
TIPPETTS
BOOK DESIGNS

www.emtippettsbookdesigns.com

Other Books By
LINDA A. MORTON

High Desert Grave Robber
The Empty Booth at Indian Market

CHAPTER 1

It's Opening Night at the opera and patrons are arriving from near and far to this hilltop gem north of Santa Fe, New Mexico. Upon reaching Opera Drive from the highway, the procession of cars and buses approach the outdoor music theater's parking lot.

It's warm on this early evening in July, though cool mountain air will set in by the second act. After exiting their vehicles, some of the patrons set up tables and chairs in the parking lot. The table settings vary, from plastic cups to fine silverware.

Part of the charm of going to the Santa Fe Opera is the view from this high vantage point. The Jemez Mountains to the west and the Sangre de Cristo Mountains to the east. For those who come early, a tailgate picnic is part of the experience.

"Do you think we'll need our shawls tonight?" asked Debra.

"Yes. It will get cool later in the evening." replied Kimberly.

As the two women walked towards the box office, they observed the parties going on around them. "Look at the tables. People have champagne, cheese and crackers and fancy desserts. Can we invite ourselves to a party?" asked Debra.

"Unless it's a table of young men, I don't think people would take too kindly to that. There are picnic boxes for sale and a restaurant inside if you're hungry."

"Well, it's my first time at the opera, so I don't know the protocol. I'm not hungry, but I am thirsty. Oh, look! There are three men at that table. Let's go talk to them." Debra exclaimed. She started towards them and her friend trailed behind reluctantly.

When they reached the men's table Debra took the lead. "Good evening, gentlemen."

"*Come sta*," replied one of the men. "How do you do."

Debra said, "Oh, that doesn't sound like Spanish. What language is that?"

"Italian. We are from Milan. *Mio nome e*, my name is Raphael. This is Gianni and Ensino." The men nodded their heads and smiled.

"How interesting. My name is Debra and this is..."

"Her friend." Debra's companion smiled.

"Would you like a glass of wine, ladies?" asked Raphael.

"Oh, that's so kind of you." Debra gushed. "This is my first opera and it looks like so much fun!"

Gianni poured two glasses half full and handed one to each of the ladies.

"Well, I think you will enjoy this one. *Cosi Fan Tutte* is a light-hearted opera. The title is Italian." he explained.

"What does the title mean in English?" Debra's friend asked.

"It means *women are like that*. The libretto, the story, is by an Italian, Lorenzo du Ponte. It takes place in 18th century Naples. The music is by Wolfgang Amadeus Mozart, an 18th century Austrian composer." replied Ensino.

"What did Lorenzo mean by saying *women are like that*?" Debra wondered aloud.

Raphael laughed. "Oh, you'll find out by the end of the opera."

The two women looked at each other and shrugged. "Thank you for the drinks, gentlemen." Debra's friend set her glass down. "We need to go pick up our tickets."

Debra was surprised at the sudden

departure and gulped down her wine. "Oh, yes, thank you. Maybe we'll see you at intermission." She left the table and followed her friend. The men waved goodbye.

"What's the hurry?" Debra asked, catching up.

"I was just thinking of Andres. I think he's going to propose soon. We've been dating for two years now and he's been dropping hints about marriage. We walked by a jewelry store in town recently and he paused to look at rings."

"Well, if that's what you want, I hope he does. I thought those men were very nice and we did get a free drink out of it." Debra laughed as the two women passed more tables of patrons drinking, eating and relishing the high mountain views.

She looked around the crowded parking lot. "This is really a great party atmosphere. I've only heard of tailgate parties at football games, not at the opera. Then again, locals say this is the *City Different*."

Kimberly slowed down, then stopped mid-gait. She squinted and her jaw dropped. She lowered her sunglasses to take another look.

Debra had kept going. She halted and turned around to see her friend standing still. "What is it?"

"Andres is here. He told me he was working tonight on a bank audit. Who is that woman with him?"

"Are you sure that's him? Where is he?" Debra had only met Andres once when he attended a house showing with Kimberly. Still, she thought she could recognize him.

"There, by the limousine. He's holding her hand. How could he!"

Debra re-positioned herself for a better look. "Oh, I see. Yes, that looks like Andres. I've seen that woman before. I think she works at the bank where I have real estate closings. What a creep to lead you on that way. If you want to go give him an earful or slap him silly, I'll back you up."

"Maybe she works with him. I don't remember seeing her." Kimberly pursed her lips in anger. "No, I won't confront him. What would he say? Oh, Debra, how could I be so naïve? How could I not know this?"

"Forget about him! Let's go get our tickets." Debra said, pulling her friend's arm.

Her friend lowered the brim of her hat as she walked with Debra to the box office. After picking up their tickets, they approached the bar.

"I'm getting a stiff drink. What will you have, Debra?"

"Just tonic with lime. I'm driving and that glass of wine was enough for me." Debra looked around the area. "Let's go stand by those people near the entrance. We can watch visitors enter the opera house, like they do on the red carpet. I'll meet you over there."

Debra joined the group along the wall

and before long, she observed a woman wearing a necklace of roses and a man wearing a long black cape.

Debra's friend joined her, sipping a martini. She handed Debra a tonic water. People were jovial as they stood in the high desert air anticipating who they would see enter at the famous opera house.

Someone nearby said "Look, there's the governor and her husband!"

"There's the red-headed actress, Shirley!" another person said.

"There's the mayor of Santa Fe and his son." Debra pointed. "Look, there's the famous British singer, Robert, wearing a tuxedo and jeans. I love his long curly hair. Who's that woman he's with? She's a lot younger than he is. I think she's a singer, too. Isn't this fun?"

"I'm getting another drink." Kimberly replied, then cut through the crowd to get to the bar. She took out her wallet to pay for her drink and felt the knife in her purse.

She'd brought it for protection, as always. She'd started carrying it after a co-worker was attacked while showing a property.

She waited for the crowd to pass then noticed Andres and his curly blonde companion strolling towards her, arm in arm. She lowered the brim of her hat and turned away slightly as the couple passed by. The woman was gazing into the man's eyes. She wore a flashy ring on her left hand.

The lights began to flicker, indicating it was time for people to take their seats. It was a ten-minute warning before the doors to the open -air theater would close until intermission.

Kimberly downed her second martini and felt her blood begin to boil. A volcanic rage ran through her veins. She saw Andres and his escort kiss, then part ways before going to the restrooms. Humiliation and jealousy consumed her now. The alcohol gave her courage. She would confront the woman.

People were dispersing and lining up to get their opera brochures from the ushers. Debra looked around for Kimberly. She had seen Andes and the other woman enter the opera house and hoped her friend didn't notice them. Debra decided to take her seat.

The angry woman strode over to the ladies' restroom. The area was nearly empty. She saw the target of her rage bragging to another woman who was washing her hands.

"I'm so happy! I got engaged tonight!" She showed off her ring as the other opera-goer dried her hands and then congratulated the jubilant woman before leaving the restroom.

Kimberly stood inside the doorway observing the interaction. The word *engaged* kept repeating in her head. She felt a pulse pounding in her temples.

While combing her hair, the excited

woman noticed someone in her peripheral vision. Someone else had entered the restroom. She pulled a tube of lipstick from her purse and smiled in the mirror. She was almost ready to meet her fiancé.

The newcomer looked under the stalls and determined there was no one else in the restroom. She took the knife out of her purse and hid it behind her skirt as she approached her target. Andres' fiancée was carefully putting on lipstick, paying no attention to anything else.

She raised the knife and pierced the unsuspecting woman's neck. There was a gasp. She stabbed again until the woman collapsed on the floor. The purse fell away from the body. The attacker stepped back to avoid blood spatter. She wrapped the purse in her skirt, careful not to get her fingerprints on it.

A rush of adrenalin gave her the strength to drag the body into a stall and lean it against one side. She locked the door and took the ring off the target's finger. The purse was shoved under the limp arm. The attacker quickly put her hat and handbag on the floor of the adjacent empty stall, then carefully slid under the divider. She flushed the toilet and opened the door. The room was still empty. The attacker grabbed paper towels and gave a quick swipe of the knife before dropping it into the trash bin.

She washed her hands and dabbed a wet paper towel with soap on the blood stain on her skirt. It was barely noticeable now. The attacker didn't see any other blood spatter on her light-colored outfit. She looked back at the stall and saw the legs. If anyone noticed, they'd think the woman had just passed out, having had too much to drink.

She adjusted her hat before leaving the restroom, making sure her face was partially obscured. She, then, walked quickly through the now- empty outdoor gathering space. Her lethal action took just under ten minutes. The usher was about to close the door when the patron pulled on the handle. She received a brochure and was quickly escorted to her seat as the lights dimmed.

Debra whispered. "I couldn't find you, so I took my seat."

The woman took off her hat and let out a long sigh. She smiled. "I just needed a little time alone. I feel better now."

The music started and the curtain rose for the first act of *Cosi Fan Tutte*.

CHAPTER 2

Nearly ninety minutes passed before the end of the first act. As the house lights brightened, the two women stood up from their seats.

"What do you think so far?" asked Debra.

"I'm glad we have the translation in English. The story is about love and infidelity. I can sure relate to that! Let's go stretch our legs. I'm going to the bar."

"I'm going to the restroom. I'll see you back here." said Debra.

On the way out of the theater, Debra noticed one of the Italian men they'd met earlier. "Hello again, Raphael. Are you enjoying the opera?"

"Very much so, and you?" he asked.

"It's kind of like a school for lovers. There's a playful experiment to see if the women will be unfaithful to their partners. The story would be lost on me if not for the translation." Debra replied.

"Yes. The translations attract more patrons to the opera. Can I get you a drink, Debra?"

"Why, yes, I'll have a tonic with lime. I need to use the restroom first. I'll be right back."

Debra hurried toward the restroom closest to her. Yellow tape was stretched across the entrance. A nervous-looking usher re-directed her to another restroom. There was a long line and some of the women were talking while waiting.

"I heard someone say a woman was

hurt in the other restroom. There are security guards in there." one woman said to another.

"Really? I hope it's nothing serious. Sometimes people have too much to drink and pass out in this high altitude." the other said in response.

Debra was surprised to hear this. People seemed to be having so much fun. She found an open stall and took care of business, then freshened up a little. On the way back to meet Raphael, she scanned the crowd and saw him.

"Here you go, Debra." He handed her the tonic with lime.

Debra sipped her drink. "Thank you. Something happened in the nearby women's restroom. I heard people talking about it."

"I'm sorry to hear that." Raphael tried to reassure her. "Let's hope no one is seriously hurt."

"You are a calming presence, Raphael."

Debra said. She looked at the sky. The sun had set and stars were appearing. "Isn't it a lovely night?"

He looked up and smiled. "Yes, it is. Debra, I will be in town for three more days. Perhaps we can meet for coffee tomorrow, *domani*? I'd like to hear your thoughts about the opera's ending. I'm staying at the Eldorado de Santa Fe, where you can reach me."

"I would like that. I'm off work tomorrow and I'd like to talk to you more about it." replied Debra.

The lights flickered, indicating it was time for patrons to return to their seats.

"*Andiamo.* Let's go." Raphael touched Debra's arm and they parted ways.

Debra found her friend already seated. "I saw that Italian man, Raphael, again. We talked and he told me where he's staying in case I want to meet for coffee."

"That's nice. Be careful, Debra. He's just visiting." her friend said.

"I know. I heard something happened in the women's restroom tonight. Security taped it off from use." Debra said.

"Really? I didn't notice."

Debra saw a red smear on the inside of her friend's blouse. She would tell her later.

The two women adjusted their electronic libretto systems on the seats before them and the lights dimmed for the second act.

CHAPTER 3

While the audience was immersed in the first act, emergency personnel were rushing to and from the restroom near the box office. A maintenance worker brought a ladder. The security guard needed it to unlock the stall door from inside.

Police were shining flashlights around the perimeter of the restroom in search of evidence.

The coroner's van arrived and parked next to the ambulance near the box office.

The paramedics had already unloaded a stretcher and life-saving equipment. They had rushed to the scene where they found the blonde woman bleeding out. The two paramedics tried to revive her, but there was no pulse. They used the Defibrillator. There was no response.

The coroner arrived and was escorted by police to the scene of the crime. The emergency personnel in the restroom were already packing up the AED and their gear. "Knife wounds to the neck. She lost a lot of blood." The paramedic continued. "We couldn't save her."

Coroner Martin Garcia put on his protective covering and gloves before checking the body on the restroom floor. He opened his black bag and took out his instruments. "Her body temperature is still warm. This victim hasn't been dead long. Maybe an hour, two at the most. The knife severed an artery and she died quickly. This looks like a crime of passion, not random."

He took out a swab and scooped up blood to put in a vial. He checked the victim's arms. He didn't see bruising. The coroner carefully lifted the hands of the deceased and scraped under her nails. He put what little he could find in another vial.

"It doesn't look like the victim fought back. You can put her on the stretcher now. We will load her in my van to take to the morgue." Coroner Garcia instructed the paramedics.

Coroner Garcia took his protective covering and gloves off while police officers and a detective searched the restroom for evidence.

The maintenance worker was asked to dismantle the main trash bin attached to the wall unit. The detective called to the scene rolled up his sleeves and put on a pair of gloves. He searched the stalls before searching the trash bin. After going through mounds of used paper towels and tissues, he felt something heavy. It was at the bottom of the trash bin. It was a knife.

"Here it is! This must be the murder weapon." The detective put the knife in an evidence bag. "Officer, take this to the Crime Lab and have it checked for prints and DNA."

Standing outside the restroom near the yellow crime scene tape was an emotionally distraught man. "My name is Andres Martinez. I don't know what happened, officer. My fiancée went into the restroom before the first act and never got to her seat. The ushers close the doors to the theater when the opera begins, so I thought she must have been too late to get inside or was in the Standing Room area. I thought I would find her at intermission."

"How did you know the victim?" asked the police officer.

"We worked together at a bank in town. I had just proposed to her tonight. She was so happy and excited. I don't know how this could happen." Andres said tearfully.

"Can someone confirm where you were during the first act?"

Andres reached into his coat pocket. "Here's my ticket. You can ask the person in the seat next to mine. I was there the entire time."

The officer called over a security guard and handed him the ticket. "Go check with the usher to see if this seat was occupied during the first act by this man."

"Can I see her? Are you sure it's her?" asked the bereaved fiancé.

"There was a purse next to the body. It had an ID in it. The victim is Janice Blaine." The officer reported. "I need you to remain here while we confirm your whereabouts."

"Yes, yes, of course." replied Mr. Martinez.

"Did your fiancée have any enemies?" asked the officer.

"Janice was a friendly and caring person. She never spoke of having any enemies."

replied Andres.

"How about you, Mr. Martinez? Would someone do this to hurt you?" inquired the officer.

The man hesitated. "I don't know, officer. I don't think so."

"We need to notify her next of kin. Can you provide that information?"

"Janice told me her family lives in Ohio. I haven't met them, but Janice said they were close. They will be heart-broken. The bank should have their contact information." responded Andres.

The officer wrote down the name of the bank, as well as the phone number and address of Andres Martinez. "Chief Romero will want to talk to you, so make yourself available the next few days."

"Yes, officer. I will. Can I see the body before you take her?" Andres pleaded. "I still can't believe this happened to my sweet Janice."

The tearful man observed the activity

going on around him. Another officer carrying a plastic bag quickly exited the crime scene. He was soon followed by a detective who was rolling down his shirt sleeves. They walked toward the parking lot where lights were flashing.

The fiancé stood frozen when he saw the black body bag on a stretcher come out of the restroom. "Please, please let me see her." Andres begged.

The officer held up his hand and stopped the stretcher. He instructed the paramedic to unzip the bag from the top. Andres Martinez saw the face of the beautiful woman he had planned to marry. Her blonde curls protruded from the bag. There was blood on her neck. "Yes, that's my dear Janice." He turned away in shock and was feeling dizzy. He leaned against a wall.

The officer signaled for the paramedic to zip the body bag and continue on.

The coroner exited with his leather case,

walking slowly behind the stretcher that carried the victim.

Nearby, a high-ranking officer was speaking to an opera representative. "We're done processing the crime scene for now. Lock the restroom and leave it as is. Keep the yellow tape up. Someone will be back in the morning. We'll let you know when it's been cleared."

"Officer, this is terrible. As long as the opera has been in existence, we've never had any criminal activity. I don't know what to tell the patrons." said the distraught representative.

"You may have to increase your security. We'll keep some officers here tonight, since the killer could still be on the opera grounds. The Sheriff sent a few deputies, too. I'll talk to the Chief about regular patrols during opera season." the officer explained before leaving the crime scene.

The outdoor area was emptying now that the emergency personnel had left.

Andres saw the security guard return and speak to the officer holding him. "The usher confirmed he sat alone during the entire first act while the seat next to his was empty."

The officer handed the ticket back to Andres. "You can go now. Someone confirmed your statement."

Andres turned to leave. The mountain air had dropped in temperature and a cool breeze caused him to shiver. He slowly exited the Santa Fe Opera House and found his car in the crowded parking lot. Once inside the vehicle, he could smell the sweet perfume that lingered in the air. He bent over the steering wheel and sobbed.

CHAPTER 4

The second act of *Cosi Fan Tutte* ended with a moral of the story in translation. *We cannot live our lives only in the moment and only for ourselves.*

Though the women fell for the trap and were unfaithful, they were forgiven and the couples joyfully reunited. The audience roared and applauded the happy ending.

There were fifteen minutes of applause for the performers and the orchestra before the house lights brightened. Patrons began to rise from their seats to leave the opera house.

"Wow! That was great!" exclaimed Debra. "What a story. It was kind of comical, but serious in a way. The women sang with such emotion! The audience really enjoyed it."

"Yes, they did." said Kimberly as she wrapped her shawl tightly around her shoulders. "I don't like the implication of the title, though. Men are unfaithful, too."

The women walked in a slow procession to leave the theater. "Well, if the story was written in the 18th century, it took a more machismo view." replied Debra.

The opera patrons dispersed into the open space where police officers now stood. Their smiles were turning into looks of concern as they left the Santa Fe Opera to return home.

"I wonder what happened? I didn't see those officers here earlier." said Debra. Her friend did not respond.

In the cool of the night, the two women

returned to their car. The roar of engines started and lines to exit the lot began to form.

"I'm so glad you offered to drive tonight, Debra. I'm feeling a little tipsy. I had a few too many martinis."

"No problem. I only had one glass of wine and tonic water. That was enough for me. It got chilly, like you said it would. I'm glad I brought my shawl." Debra looked over at her friend, who had tears streaming down her face. "What's wrong?"

"Oh, I'm just feeling emotional. This opera was about infidelity and after seeing Andres with that woman, I'm, I'm just so sad." Her friend began to sob.

Before entering busy Opera Drive, Debra looked at Kimberly. "Forget about him. He's not worth it and he can't be trusted."

"I know, I know." The woman replied before laying her head against the car window. Her eyes were closed.

Debra drove in silence as her car

approached the highway. She felt badly for her new friend and hoped she would feel better in the morning. The woman sitting next to her was a top producer in the real estate business and to see her so vulnerable was unexpected.

While driving, Debra's thoughts shifted to pondering what might have happened in the ladies' restroom tonight that brought such a police presence.

CHAPTER 5

This Saturday morning, Laura Bennett came back from walking her dogs in the village of La Cienega. The cool summer morning was a good time to take a walk in her new neighborhood. She picked up the Santa Fe Journal and a few pastries from the village store on her way.

It had been six months since she and Agent Marc Bennett got married. They bought the adobe house before the marriage and took their time before moving in. Between her teaching schedule and his FBI work, they wanted time to make home repairs before settling in.

Laura fed the dogs and looked for her husband. He was working in the yard. "What do you want to do today?" asked Laura.

"Oh, I don't know. I haven't had a day off in well over a week, so I wouldn't mind staying home." replied Marc.

"I picked up the Santa Fe Journal when I was out, so I'll see what's happening in town tonight. I'll make some eggs and potatoes for breakfast. I'll see you inside."

Laura got breakfast ready, along with a bowl of green chile. She fried some bacon and warmed the tortillas to create her own version of *huevos rancheros*, a rancher's breakfast. She tried to make it like the hotel restaurant in town, their favorite breakfast spot.

Marc entered the kitchen and washed his hands. He joined his wife at the table and began eating. "It tastes good, Laura. You're perfecting our favorite breakfast. You really are a good cook. We ate out a lot when we were dating and I didn't realize it until we moved in together."

"Thank you, agent. You know, when I eat a meal at a restaurant that I really like, I try to duplicate it at home. That's what I did with meatloaf. We had the Santa Fe Meatloaf at the Purple Adobe when we met during the gallery investigation, remember? I really liked it and I figured out the ingredients. The proportions change a little, but I use the same ingredients as the restaurant."

"That's very creative. It's just one of the things I love about you." Marc smiled at his wife and finished his breakfast. He gathered his empty plate and went to the sink. He noticed the pastries on the counter top and decided to save one for later.

Laura picked up the newspaper and

saw the headline, ***Murder at the Opera***. *A young woman was murdered at the Santa Fe Opera Friday evening. The police aren't releasing her name until they notify the next of kin. At this time, there are no suspects in custody. If someone has any information, they are to call the Santa Fe Police.*

Laura looked serious. "Marc, there was a murder at the opera. I've heard that Opening Night is quite a festive occasion. That was last night. It's horrible for the victim and for the opera." Laura said.

"Yes, this is very unfortunate for all involved."

"I had always wanted to go to the Santa Fe Opera. I used to go to the Chicago Lyric Opera when I lived there." Laura said.

"I'm not a big fan of opera but I've heard the Santa Fe Opera is world class. It's unusual because it's an open- air theater on a hilltop. It must have great views. Why don't you get us some tickets for tonight?" Marc said.

"Really? Well, they can sure use the support now with this news. Let me see what's playing tonight." She turned to the Events page of the paper. "*Cosi Fan Tutte*. It's an Italian opera. I've heard there are screens at each seat to translate the language into English or Spanish. Shall I call the box office?" Laura asked.

"Yes, go ahead. I'm going to take it easy today since it will be a late night." Marc replied.

"I'll get tickets, then I need to look for something nice to wear." Laura paused. "You know, Marc, this is the same opera that was performed last night. The night of the murder."

Agent Marc Bennett had a feeling he should call Santa Fe Police Chief Romero, with whom he sometimes worked on cases.

"I'll give Chief Romero a call. I'll let him know we're going in case he wants me involved."

CHAPTER 6

Chief Romero went to his office on this Saturday morning. After getting some fresh coffee and a donut from the station's kitchen, he spoke to his sergeant. "I'll need the Police Report on the opera murder last night."

"Yes, Sir." the sergeant replied.

The Police Report arrived within minutes and the Chief took out his pen and notepad. *A waitress, Angela Moreno, found the body in the women's restroom during act one. The body was in a stall laying in a pool of blood. She called security. The stall door was locked and they needed a ladder to open it from inside. Local police were on the scene within minutes. The victim was Janice Blaine, a local banker. She came to the opera with Andres Martinez, phone #... He proposed to her last night. Knife was found in the restroom trash bin by detective on scene. Coroner says victim was stabbed in the neck. Appears to be a crime of passion. No suspects. No witnesses.*

The Police Chief called in the sergeant. "Who is the detective working the case?"

"Roger Stewart worked the case last night. He found the knife in the trash bin and put it into evidence to check for prints and DNA."

"Good. Have the detective call me." the Chief instructed.

"Sir, Detective Stewart called in this morning to say his wife was in labor at the hospital. When he got home from the crime scene last night, he had to take her in. It's been a long night." the sergeant explained.

"OK, I understand. Call this man Andres Martinez. Tell him to come to the station for an interview." instructed the Chief.

The Chief got a call. "Chief Romero, this is Agent Bennett with the FBI. I just read about the murder at the opera last night."

"Yes, agent, I was just reading the report."

"I wanted to let you know that Laura and I plan to go to the Santa Fe Opera tonight. It's something she always wanted to do. I thought I would look around and ask a few questions, if it's all right with you."

"Well, agent, it's good timing. I just learned that the detective on the scene last night is unavailable for a few days. Maybe you and Laura can go early before the opera opens to the public and interview some of the staff. A waitress, Angela Moreno, found the body and alerted Opera Security. I'll call the Opera House and tell them you're coming. They should get you a list of employees who worked last night. I'm sending a patrol car out there tonight and every night through the opera season. In all my years in Santa Fe, I've never heard of a crime at this Opera House."

"We'll get there early so I have time to interview staff."

"You're a great help, Agent Bennett. I'll call the FBI office and inform Agent Garland that you're assisting us here. In the meantime, I'm going to interview the victim's fiancé. He just proposed to her last night before the murder. I wonder if that's a coincidence. According to the coroner's notes, this appears to be a crime of passion, not a random act of violence."

"I'll give you an update tomorrow, Chief." the agent responded before ending the call.

Chief Romero dialed the Coroner's Office. "This is Police Chief Romero. I need an update on the report for Janice Blaine." The Chief was put on hold then heard the familiar voice of Martin Garcia, the County Coroner.

"Hello Chief. I was just finishing my report. The knife cut an artery and she bled out. There were two knife entry wounds. There were no defensive wounds. She must have been attacked from behind and taken by surprise. She was dragged over to the stall and propped up against the wall, where she was found. She was still warm when I arrived, so only dead an hour or two, at the most."

"Did you find any DNA on her clothes? Was she wearing any jewelry?" asked the Chief.

"There was blood on her clothes, which matches her own DNA. She wore earrings and a bracelet. I'm having them checked for prints." replied the coroner.

"Did she have a ring on?"

"No. There were no rings."

"Interesting." said the Chief.

"Why is that?"

"She got engaged last night, so she would have worn an engagement ring. I'll verify that with her fiancé, who's coming in for an interview. Send me your report when completed. And Martin, do you think a woman could have committed this crime?" asked the Chief.

"The victim was petite, about 5 feet 3 inches and slim. A taller woman, heavier woman could have done this, yes." replied the coroner.

"OK, thanks Martin." The Chief put down the receiver. He made a note: no engagement ring.

Chief Romero finished his coffee and called the Sheriff's Department. "Sheriff Jones, this is Santa Fe Police Chief Romero. Did you have anyone at the opera last night?"

"Yes, Chief, we had two deputies there. One for the governor and one for the mayor." answered the Sheriff.

"Where were they stationed during the

performance?" asked the Chief.

"They stayed in the Standing Room area within eyesight of the dignitaries. Why do you ask?"

"Can you ask them if they noticed anyone coming in late to the first act? The murder victim was killed just before or during the beginning of the first act."

"That's a good point. I'll follow-up with them." said Sheriff Jones.

"And Sheriff, I'm sending a patrol car to the opera every night during the opera season. If you can spare a deputy, maybe we can reassure the guests. They can coordinate with opera security."

"Of course. We have a killer on the loose. Keep me posted on your findings, Chief."

Chief Romero knew that patrons came from around the world to see the Santa Fe Opera. People traveled in and out of town on a regular basis during the opera season. He hoped the murder suspect didn't already leave town.

The police sergeant entered the office. "Sir, Mr. Martinez is here."

"OK. Take him to the Interrogation Room. I'll be right there." The Chief gathered his notebook and pen. He walked into the room and turned on the video camera.

"Mr. Martinez, I'm Chief Romero. Thank you for coming in today."

The man nodded his head. His shoulders were slumped and he looked tired.

"Tell me about you and Janice Blaine." the Chief began.

The visitor put his hands on the table and folded them. He took a deep breath and sat up straight. "I worked with Janice at the bank in town. We became close this past year and I proposed to her last night before the opera. We had a picnic in the parking lot where other parties were taking place. We went inside the Opera House and we both needed to use the restroom, so we parted." Andres lowered his head. "We kissed goodbye. The lights flickered and we needed to get to our seats. I went on ahead, expecting Janice to follow. She never came. At intermission, I looked for her by the restroom and saw the yellow tape. I told the officer I was looking for Janice. That's when I learned she was killed."

"Did you give Janice an engagement ring?" The Chief asked.

The visitor smiled. "Yes, I did. It fit perfectly. She really loved it." His smile quickly faded.

"Mr. Martinez, can you think of anyone who would want to do this to Janice? Did she have an ex-husband or former boyfriend who might want to harm her?"

"Janice was kind and sweet. She was good with people. She never indicated she had any enemies. She was never married and told me she rarely dated anyone more than a few weeks until we met."

"How about you? Do you have enemies?" asked the Chief.

Andres wrung his hands. He appeared nervous while looking down at the table.

"Is there something you want to tell me, Mr. Martinez? Is there someone who may want retaliation for something you did?"

The man grimaced and averted his eyes. "I'm not proud of it, but I was dating another woman while I was seeing Janice."

"Tell me about that." directed the Chief.

"I was dating a woman here, in town. We met two years ago. She's a real estate broker who sometimes did closings at the bank I work at."

"What's her name?" the Chief inquired.

"Kimberly. Kimberly Montoya." replied Andres.

"Did Kimberly know about Janice and vice versa?"

"I don't think so. Everything was strictly business at the bank. I never told anyone at work who I was dating. I don't think Janice was aware I was seeing Kimberly or vice versa."

Chief Romero wanted to follow this lead. "Have you ever seen Kimberly get angry or violent?"

"I've seen her get irritated at other drivers on the road. She got angry once when a real estate deal fell apart. I've never seen her anger directed towards me or someone I know."

"You said you met Kimberly two years ago. When was the last time you spoke with her?"

"Earlier in the week. We met for dinner on Monday night." Andres answered.

"Did you indicate you were breaking up with her? Did you tell her you were seeing another woman?"

"I was going to, but couldn't. I was just going to stop taking her calls until I found the right time to break it off. Like I said, I'm not proud of it." Andres hung his head in embarrassment.

"Mr. Martinez, do you know if Kimberly went to the opera last night?" the Chief continued.

The man raised his head and dropped his jaw as he stared at the Chief. "Oh no. On Monday, she asked if I'd like to go to the Opening Night with her. I said I had to work late to do an audit. That was just an excuse I made up. I didn't work late. Oh no..."

"Did you see Kimberly last night?"

"No, I didn't. I wasn't looking at anyone but Janice. We were in love." his voice trailed off.

"What office does Kimberly work in? Write down her address and phone number." the Chief directed. "Another thing, how tall is Kimberly?"

"She's about 5'8. I'm 6 feet and she's a little shorter than I am." replied Andres.

"Mr. Martinez, there was no engagement ring found on the victim. People don't usually kill for a piece of jewelry. The victim's bracelet and earrings were still intact." The Chief let out a deep sigh.

"There's an old saying. *Love hath no fury like that of a woman scorned.*"

"Wait here while I make a call." the Chief instructed Mr. Martinez.

Chief Romero returned to his office and accessed the Department of Motor Vehicles data network. He entered the name Kimberly Montoya and requested her driver's license and vehicle information.

Within minutes, he pulled up photos, addresses and vehicle information of three women with the same name. He printed out the information and returned to the room where Mr. Martinez anxiously waited.

Chief Romero set the photos on the table. "Can you identify any of these women?"

The man looked closely at the photos and pointed to one. "Yes, that's Kimberly."

"Is this her current address as listed on her license?"

"Yes, that's her house." replied Mr. Martinez.

"OK, you can go now. Let me know if

you hear from Kimberly." The Chief gave his card to the man.

"And Mr. Martinez, I'd be careful if I were you."

CHAPTER 7

After a late night out, Debra slept in longer than usual. By the time she took her tipsy friend home and got to her condo on Old Pecos Trail, it was one thirty a.m.

It was now nine thirty on Saturday morning. She made her morning coffee and turned on the local news station. The weather would be near ninety degrees today, with an afternoon storm coming in. Then, breaking news. *'A woman was found murdered at the Santa Fe Opera Friday night. It was the Opening Night at the Opera and the theater was filled. The identity of the victim is being withheld. No one is in custody. If you have any information, call Santa Fe Police.'*

Debra's hand started shaking and her coffee was spilling over the brim. She set it down for a minute and took a deep breath. She was just there. She was just there at the scene of the murder.

Debra decided to call her friend. The phone rang five times before a groggy voice answered. "Hello."

"This is Debra. Did you hear the news? A woman was murdered at the opera last night!"

"Really?" The voice was groggy. "I have a splitting headache. I'll call you later." The friend hung up.

Debra decided to call the Eldorado de Santa Fe. "Can I have the room for Raphael, the guest from Milan? I don't know his last name." She was soon connected and heard the charming voice.

"Raphael, this is Debra from the opera. Can we meet for brunch today? I have so much to talk to you about."

"Yes, Debra. I'm glad you called. The hotel has a lovely brunch menu. Can we meet in an hour?"

"Yes. I'll meet you in the lobby."

Debra finished drinking her coffee and took a quick shower. By the time she got dressed, it was ten fifteen. She got in her car and drove downtown. She would be a little late.

After parking in the lot down the street, Debra entered the grand entrance to the hotel. It was a lovely lobby with high ceilings. She had sometimes met real estate clients here from out of town.

Raphael stood to greet her. "It's so good to see you again, Debra." They shook hands, then walked into the spacious restaurant.

The host seated them. A waiter

approached and took their orders. Raphael smiled and asked "So, Debra, how did you like the ending of the opera?"

"Well, the women fell for the trap, but it could work the other way, you know. Men can be unfaithful, too. The partners forgave the women for being unfaithful, which is hard to do in real life. I guess Lorenzo thought only women were prone to temptation when he wrote that libretto." Debra reasoned.

"You have a point. He took a serious topic of infidelity and tried to make a comedy. The music of Mozart helped to lighten the mood. The soprano expressed her emotional turmoil very well, don't you think? It must be quite a challenge to sing at 7000 feet elevation." Raphael responded in his Italian accent.

"Yes, they need to acclimate to this elevation." Debra replied. "You know, it was a coincidence that my friend and I attended this opera on the very night she discovered her boyfriend was being unfaithful. She really felt betrayed. It must have been very difficult for her to see the humor in the opera. She had a few drinks and cried afterwards. I called her this morning, but she didn't want to talk." Debra explained.

Their food arrived and they began to eat. "I have observed through life that some people can handle emotional turmoil better than others. Some can brush it off and move on, while others succumb to anger and rage or depression. Betrayal is actually a common theme in many famous operas." said the Italian companion.

"I hope my friend can brush it off. I don't know her very well. We're both real estate brokers from different offices. When I mentioned I'd like to attend an opera, Kimberly suggested we go to the Opening Night. She had wanted to go with her boyfriend, but he said he was working late. Then, there he was, partying with another woman. They seemed very romantic, too.

My friend was fuming when she saw them."

"Yes, that must have hurt. The opera might have been difficult for her to watch because of that experience. Like I said, some people can brush it off and others can't." Raphael said.

They finished their meals and commented on the food and atmosphere.

"What do you do for a living in Milan?" asked Debra.

"*Sono maestro.* I am a high school teacher. I teach History. Since I love opera, I teach an elective class in Opera Appreciation, as well." Raphael said proudly.

"That's interesting. If I had an opera class like that in my high school, I would have signed up for it."

"I believe opera is one of the noblest art forms and I enjoy introducing it to young people." replied Raphael.

"You have a calm demeanor. I imagine your students must enjoy your classes." Debra smiled, then changed the subject.

"Raphael, there was something in the local news this morning. I don't know if you've heard. A woman was murdered at the opera last night."

Raphael's pleasant mood changed. "No, you can't be serious! I have never heard of such a thing happening at an Opera House!" He put his hand to his forehead in shock, then reflected. "Debra, last night when I saw you at the intermission, you said the women's restroom was blocked off so it must have happened before we met. Patrons are discouraged from leaving their seats during the opera."

Raphael shook his head in disbelief. "I have been to many of the world's Opera Houses and never heard of any criminal activity. This is tragic, Debra, in many ways."

"I know. A young woman was killed. The name hasn't been released yet. When we were leaving last night, I noticed police officers around the premises. I didn't see an ambulance, so they must have carried her out during the first act."

Raphael let out a deep sigh. "We noticed the police presence, as well. I will tell Gianni and Ensino. They will be shocked, as I am. It is so tragic that a murder would occur at one of the most festive events of the year in Santa Fe. Opening Night is the highlight of the opera season. I am very upset to hear this, Debra. Let's go for a walk, shall we?" Raphael paid the tab and they stood up to leave.

"Yes, I would like that." Debra agreed.

They stepped outside into the glaring sunlight and slowly walked the streets of downtown Santa Fe. Tourists were already filling the sidewalks as the pair strolled down San Francisco Street. The St. Francis Cathedral came into view.

"I would like to go to the Cathedral. I need to renew my spirit after hearing this shocking news. Will you join me?" the Italian companion suggested.

"Yes, I would like to say a prayer." Debra replied. She was glad she wasn't alone and could discuss these events with Raphael. As they walked, there was something tugging at the back of her mind. She couldn't remember what it was.

CHAPTER 8

After taking a couple of pain relievers for her headache, Kimberly took a cold shower. She didn't want to remember the Friday night before. There was so much heartache. Her jealousy had consumed her and she had too much to drink.

After a cup of tea and toast, she made a decision. She would go out of town for a few days. She looked at her schedule. She had three showings set for Sunday with a home buyer. She would call the office and arrange for another broker to take the clients out. Kimberly was a top agent in the office and newer agents enjoyed doing favors for her, even on short notice. She would pay them for their time and they would get some experience. She sent a text to her clients informing them of the change.

She put on her jeans and blouse, then the brunette grabbed a suitcase and packed up some clothes for three days. She would stop at the ATM for some cash. She made up a bag of snacks to keep in the car, then watered the plants.

It was eleven a.m. She looked at her New Mexico road map and decided to drive north to Taos. She put on her favorite baseball cap, locked the door and waved to her neighbors. The older couple was sitting on their porch and watched as their neighbor backed out of her driveway.

Kimberly filled up her black Mercedes sedan with gas then proceeded to the

ATM. She withdrew as much money as the machine allowed. Upon entering her car, she took St. Francis Drive out of town and merged onto Highway 84/285. There was steady traffic in both directions on this Saturday in July. To her left, she saw the rooftop of the opera house. On the right, she saw the exit to Opera Drive.

She felt a pit in her stomach. It had been about fifteen hours since she saw the couple. Though she was mad at Andres, she still cared about him. Maybe she would hear from him. He would get lonely and come back to her.

As she drove, she thought about what she did with the ring. Though she was drowsy, she recalled putting her beaded purse in the desk drawer. The ring was in the purse. Upon returning from Taos, she'll look for the ring.

For now, Kimberly Montoya would concentrate on driving and listening to music. It was a beautiful day in New Mexico and she wanted to live in the moment. She didn't want any negative thoughts. She sang along with the music on the radio and let her long brown hair blow in the wind.

CHAPTER 9

"You look lovely, my dear." Marc said admiringly to his new bride.

Laura was wearing a long black dress and her favorite turquoise necklace and earrings. Her flowered shawl was something she'd bought at a flamenco festival in Santa Fe.

"Thank you, Agent Bennett. You look dashing yourself." Laura appreciated her husband's sense of fashion. He wore a black blazer over pressed jeans, a turquoise bolo tie over a crisp white shirt, a sterling silver Ranger Set and black boots. Laura kissed him gently before leaving the house.

It was five o'clock on this Saturday evening. They drove north on Interstate 25 to St. Francis Drive then merged onto Highway 84/285. Marc and Laura were having a big night out, but they had an objective.

"I have a small notepad and pen to take notes if I hear something useful to the case." Laura said.

"Good. I have a notepad in my jacket. The Chief sent me a photo of a person of interest, a woman. I'll forward the photo to your phone when we arrive. We'll stop at the box office for tickets and get the list of employees who worked last night. I'm looking for a waitress, Angela Moreno. She found the body." said Marc.

"I'll stroll around and check to see which ushers worked the doors." said Laura.

"Let's meet up at the restaurant for

dinner. Shall we say seven?"

"OK. I'll make a reservation for seven." Laura replied.

They took the exit to Opera Drive and found a parking space close to the box office. It was just past five thirty and few patrons had arrived. The agent opened his console and took out his FBI badge. He would keep his firearm locked in its' case. He wasn't expecting to need it. He forwarded the photo to Laura's phone, as promised.

Then, Marc went to the passenger door and opened it for his wife. She held out her hand for him. "I hope you enjoy the opera. It's supposed to be about infidelity, something I hope to never experience."

"Of course not. I promise." He held her hand as they walked to the box office.

When they got there, he showed his badge. "I'm Agent Marc Bennett. I'm picking up two tickets for my wife and I. Chief Romero said you would have a list of staff who worked last night. Can you tell me where I can find Angela Moreno?"

The office manager handed him a list and two tickets. "She works at the first bar. There is another bar further back. Angela should be there shortly. The waitresses help prep the bar, so they're here early."

"How about the ushers? Are they here yet?" asked Marc.

"The ushers come in a little later, six thirty."

"Where will I find them?"

"Inside the theater near the doors. They unwrap boxes of opera brochures to hand out to patrons. Patrons can be seated at seven, if they want, so ushers are at the door by then."

"Are the same security guards on duty tonight? I'd like to speak to the guard who found the victim."

"I'll have to get back to you on that. The guards rotate. Check back at intermission."

"OK. Thanks. My wife and I plan to

have dinner at seven, so I will conduct my interviews beforehand."

Marc gave Laura her ticket. "I'll catch up with you later." Laura said. Marc nodded, then turned towards the opera house.

Laura strolled the grounds. She noticed the women's restroom was open and went inside to freshen up. There was a staff member inside. They greeted one another.

"I'm so glad this one's open again." the woman said. "It was closed off last night. There were long lines at the other restrooms."

"Why was it closed off?" asked Laura, though she already knew.

"It was a crime scene. Today's paper had an article about it." the woman said.

"I read that, now that you mention it. It's really horrible. How is the staff handling it?" Laura asked.

"Some of us talked about it last night, since police and paramedics were here. They're saying the opera has increased security around the grounds. We'll try to just focus on our work and hope our patrons have a good time." The staffer smiled and left the restroom.

Laura looked in the empty stalls. One of the stalls had been the scene of the crime last night. She didn't know which one. The place had been processed, then scrubbed by opera maintenance. Laura looked around inside the stalls when she noticed a small piece of paper tucked behind a porcelain bowl. She got a paper towel and lifted it. It was part of a ticket. She wrapped it in the paper and put it in her purse. She would give it to Marc in case it was related to the crime.

She continued walking the grounds and peaked inside the theater. There was a high white slanted rooftop and the sides were open to the air. Laura had read that the unusually designed roof covering collected rainwater that was stored and used to water the opera grounds.

She walked towards the front entrance and saw Marc talking to a woman at the bar. He was showing her a photo on his phone. The woman nodded her head, not recognizing the face. Marc took notes of their conversation.

Laura proceeded to the outdoor restaurant covered by a long portal. She found a hostess. "I'd like to make a dinner reservation for two at seven. The name is Bennett."

She noticed a bar was setting up and walked over. "Can I get a glass of cranberry juice and tonic, please?" She paid the waiter and looked around. The evening was still warm and she saw a string of vehicles approaching the opera parking lot. It was a little after six now.

Laura decided to go back to the parking lot where she found more cars parked and tables and chairs being set up. She had heard about the tailgate picnics here. She strolled through some of the rows of tables as she sipped her drink. She would never see this at the Chicago Lyric Opera. She stopped to take a photo of the festive area with her phone. She would send it to her father, an opera fan, in Chicago.

Shadows were beginning to form on the mountain range. Laura decided to go back inside and look for the ushers. She saw that Marc was talking to a waiter at the bar now, still taking notes. It was six thirty. She tossed her plastic cup in the recycle bin and went inside the theater. There were men and women opening boxes. She approached one of the women.

"Excuse me. My husband is with the FBI and he's interviewing some of the staff who might have witnessed something last night. Did you see anyone leave during the first act?" Laura asked politely.

"I didn't see anything unusual. Most patrons were in their seats by the start of the first act and no one left in my area. You can ask the others." replied the usher.

Laura approached another usher and introduced herself. "Did you see anyone come in late for the first act or leave early?"

"Well, actually, yes. I remember that I was about to close the door and someone pulled it open. A woman in a hat. I escorted her to her seat and gave her a brochure." the female usher said.

"Do you happen to remember where her seat was? Can you show me?" asked Laura.

The usher put the brochures she was holding down on the seat closest to her and walked down the aisle. She stopped at Row L. "It was this row and one of these seats close to the aisle, maybe seat 3 or 4."

Laura wrote down the row and seat numbers. "Can I have your name? Agent Bennett is interviewing staff tonight and he has a photo he'd like to show you. Do you think you'd recognize the woman?"

"I am Louisa Tomas. My number is...... I'll be working the entire opera season, so they can always find me here. I don't know if I'd recognize her. The hat obscured her face with its wide brim. I left before she took it off. We ask that patrons remove their hats before the opera begins."

"Thanks for your help, Louisa. Agent Bennett will look for you at Intermission." Laura thanked the usher and left the theater.

It was near seven, so Laura walked over to the restaurant. She was escorted to her table and ordered a glass of red wine for herself and tonic water with lemon for her husband.

The restaurant was now bustling with opera patrons. Laura looked out at the mountain views while she waited for her husband to arrive. It was a spectacular hilltop setting. Shades of purple, pink and red were covering the hills now. The colorful mountains stood in contrast to the turquoise blue sky. Sunset was slowly approaching. Laura never tired of New

Mexico sunsets.

Within minutes, her husband was in view. "I'm glad you ordered drinks. What looks good on the menu?" he asked.

"I haven't even looked at the menu." Laura laughed. "I've just been admiring the mountains."

The waiter approached and relayed the specials of the day.

"It all looks good." said Laura. "I'd like some seafood. I'll have the Scallops and a Caesar Salad."

"I'll have Pot Roast. I haven't had that in a while." Marc ordered and drank the refreshing tonic water. The waiter left and Marc looked out at the mountain view. "It really is a beautiful view." He looked at Laura.

"Did you talk to Angela, the waitress?" asked Laura.

"I did. She said she used the restroom soon after the first act had started. The staff waits until the opera begins before taking their breaks. She noticed someone's legs on the floor in a stall. She looked under the door and saw blood. She tried to open the door, but it was locked. She ran out to tell security." Marc explained.

"I saw you talking to a waiter. What did he say?" Laura asked while sipping her wine.

"I asked if he noticed anyone at the bar who looked upset or angry. He said he did notice a woman who seemed mad about something. Most people were jovial and excited at the opera, so she stood out to him. She ordered double martinis and drank them pretty quickly. When I asked for a description, he said she might be Anglo or Latino, with long brown hair. Late thirties, early forties." Marc said as he finished his tonic water. "I showed him the photo the Chief sent me. He couldn't be certain since they didn't make eye contact and the woman wore a wide brimmed hat."

The waiter approached with their meals

and Marc ordered two more drinks.

"Well, I have something for you. I found a piece of a ticket behind the stall in the women's restroom. I wrapped it in a paper towel. Maybe it was from the suspect or the victim? I have it in my purse." Laura said before tasting her scallops.

"That's interesting, Laura. We can use it as possible evidence."

They commented on their delicious meals and the mountains that were changing colors.

"I, also, spoke to some of the ushers. One woman named Louisa said something interesting. She said that just before the first act was set to begin, a woman pulled the door open as Louisa was closing it. She escorted the woman to Row L. She told me what the seat numbers might be. I wrote them down. She said the woman was wearing a wide-brimmed hat. I told her you'd like to show her a photo at intermission." Laura explained.

"OK. We're getting some good information. I still want to talk to the security guard who was called to the scene. I'll check the box office again and find the usher at intermission." Marc looked at his watch. It was seven forty -five. "We'd better get to our seats." He paid the bill and the couple left the restaurant.

Laura observed uniformed officers stationed near the bar and restrooms. "There's certainly a police presence here."

An usher escorted them to their aisle seats. "I'm so excited! I hope you like it, Marc." Laura said.

"I'm just glad to be here with you." Marc said as he reached for his wife's hand.

CHAPTER 10

Earlier on Saturday, Chief Romero had instructed two officers to go to the home of Kimberly Montoya. Based on what the grieving fiancé said, if Kimberly was at the opera on Opening Night and happened to see him with another woman, she would be a person of interest. They needed to know her whereabouts on the night of the murder.

The officers pulled into the driveway of the suspect's home at twelve thirty. They observed an older couple at the house next door sitting in chairs on their porch. The officers exited their vehicle and approached Kimberly Montoya's front door. They rang the bell three times. No one answered.

The male officer went around the back and entered the yard through a gate. He saw a patio with sliding glass doors. He walked up to the doors and peered inside, then knocked. Again, no one responded. He went around to join his partner in the front. "Nothing. No movement inside. No lights on."

The female officer went next door to speak to the couple on the porch. "*Hola! Habla ingles?*"

"*Si.* Yes, Officer." the woman replied as the other officer joined them.

"I'm Officer Corrina and this is Officer Stephen."

"Did you see your neighbor, Miss Montoya today? We need to speak to her."

"Yes, we saw her a little while ago. She had a suitcase and put it in her car. She waved at us." said the older man.

"Do you know about what time she left?" asked Officer Stephen.

The woman responded. "Maybe eleven. We had just come out on the porch at ten forty-five. We saw her leave soon after that."

Officer Corrina took out her card, walked onto the porch and handed the card to the man. "If you see her, please call this number. Can I have your names?"

"Rosa and Marco Reyes. We have lived here many years. Is Kimberly in trouble?" asked Rosa.

"No, we just want to talk to her. Did she seem upset about anything that you noticed?" Officer Stephen inquired.

"No. She just seemed like she was in a hurry." responded Marco.

"Thank you for your time, Mr. and Mrs. Reyes." Officer Corrina said. The officers returned to their vehicle.

"Let's go to the real estate office."

suggested Corrina." See if they know where she might have gone."

The officers drove to the building located on Palace Avenue. While her partner called Chief Romero from the vehicle, Officer Corrina went inside.

"Is Kimberly Montoya working today?" she asked.

The secretary called someone else in the office to respond. A couple of minutes later, a man in a suit came to the front.

"I am the managing broker. Can I help you?" he asked.

"I'm looking for Kimberly Montoya. I was told she worked here. I need to ask her some questions." Officer Corrina responded.

"She's not in the building at the moment. The brokers come and go on their own schedules. They're independent contractors and not on a salary. I did hear that Kimberly asked another broker to take her clients out on Sunday. Sometimes, brokers get busy and ask others to assist. No one's required to explain why as long as someone else works with their clients."

"Can you reach the broker and ask if Miss Montoya said why she couldn't work on Sunday? That would be helpful."

"I can try. Would you like to wait in my office?"

"No, I'll wait here."

The manager left the reception area. Officer Corrina looked around. The lobby was nicely decorated and the building was situated in a good location near the Plaza.

"Do you have a photo of Miss Montoya?" she asked the secretary.

"Yes. We have photos of all our brokers. I'll print one out for you." The secretary looked at her computer screen and pushed some buttons. After a minute, she picked up a sheet of paper from the printer nearby. "Here you go." She handed it to the officer.

"Thank you." Officer Corrina looked at the color photo. Miss Montoya had long brown hair and an attractive face.

The managing broker returned. "Apparently, Kimberly went out of town for a few days. The broker wasn't told where Kimberly was going. They just made an arrangement to show specific properties to the clients and where to meet them. That's all I can tell you."

"Here's my card." Officer Corrina took one out of her shirt pocket and handed it to him. "If either of you see Miss Montoya or learn anything on her location, call that number. Thanks for your cooperation."

She went back outside and got into the patrol car. "I've got a good photo of the suspect. Let's go to the station. The Chief may want to send out a BOLO."

Officer Stephen nodded. The patrol car left the real estate office and headed to the Lincoln Avenue Station.

The two officers entered the building and went to see their boss. "Chief, Kimberly Montoya was not at home or her office."

Corrina began. "Her neighbors said she left around eleven this morning carrying a suitcase. Her office said she was leaving town for a few days. I got a photo from the secretary." She handed the photo to the Chief.

"OK, Officer. The Department of Motor Vehicles gave me Miss Montoya's license plate and VIN numbers. She's driving a black Mercedes four door sedan. Go back and patrol her house unless you get another service call. So far, she's our only lead."

After the two officers left, Chief Romero set the photo on his desk and snapped a picture of it. Then, he called in his sergeant and gave him the original. "Put out a BOLO along with the vehicle information. Kimberly Montoya may still be in New Mexico. When she's found, bring her in for questioning. So far, she's still a person of interest."

"Yes, sir."

The sergeant left to take care of the BOLO. It was now two p.m. Chief Romero texted the photo to Agent Bennett. *This woman may have been at the opera Friday night. She was, also, dating the victim's fiancé. Connection?*

CHAPTER 11

It was the end of the first act and the audience applauded for five minutes before leaving their seats for intermission.

"How do you like it, Marc?" Laura asked.

"I really enjoy the music of Mozart. The story is rather comical. Two men testing their girlfriends to see if they'll be unfaithful."

"Yes, we'll see how that turns out. I think it should be the other way around. I think the women should test the men."

Laura replied as they exited the theater.

"Laura, take me to the usher you spoke to. I want to show her the photo, then I need to get to the box office." Marc said as they walked through the crowd of patrons.

"I'll take you to her door. I think it's the next one over. Her name is Louisa."

"Laura, I'll meet you back at our seats. Thanks for your help." Marc said as he took out his phone. He turned it on and found the photo.

Marc found the usher standing inside the door to the theater. "Excuse me, Louisa?"

"Yes, that's me."

"I'm Agent Bennett. My wife said you seated a woman last night who came in late for the first act. Can I show you a photo?'

"Yes."

Marc showed the usher the photo. "The woman was wearing a wide hat, so I didn't see her eyes. The nose and mouth look the same and she had long brown hair, like your photo."

"OK, thank you, Louisa." Marc said. He left the theater and turned towards the box office. The manager was in. "Do you have any information on that security guard from last night?"

"Yes, I have his name and phone number for you. He's not working tonight."

"Another thing. Do you have a record of a Kimberly Montoya buying opera tickets for last night?" asked the agent.

"Give me a minute." The manager sat down at a computer and searched receipts for the night before.

"No, I don't have her name in the system for last night." replied the office manager.

"Do you have her on record for past purchases?" asked Marc.

The manager scanned the computer data. "Yes, she purchased tickets last year."

"I'll need her credit card number."

"Oh, I don't know about that. It's personal

information." responded the manager.

"Look, right now, this woman is a person of interest in a murder investigation. We're trying to track her whereabouts and this card number can help us locate her. I can issue a warrant for it or you can give it to me now." Agent Bennett insisted.

The manager pondered what to do, then reluctantly wrote down the card number she saw on the screen. She handed over the piece of paper.

"OK, thanks for your help." Marc put the paper in his coat pocket. Returning to the theater, he looked for the closest men's restroom. He wanted to freshen up before the start of the second act.

As he walked the opera grounds, he wondered about the suspect. If she didn't buy the tickets, who did?

The lights began to flicker. He got to his seat just in time.

CHAPTER 12

After leaving the St. Francis Cathedral, Debra and Raphael sat on a bench in the Santa Fe Plaza. Debra felt better after saying a prayer. Just being in the beautiful cathedral was inspiring.

"Oh, there are your friends, Raphael. They're window-shopping."

"Yes, they wanted to find some turquoise to take back to Milan. Gianni likes the men's Bolo ties and Ensino is looking for cuff links." he replied.

"Are they teachers, like you?" Debra asked.

"*Si*. Yes, we teach at the same high school. Gianni teaches Math and Ensino teaches Music. We all like to travel, so decided to make this trip together. They will be saddened when I tell them what happened last night."

Debra looked out at the people walking by, then remembered something. The red stain on her friend's blouse. She forgot to mention it last night. Debra took her phone out of her purse.

"Excuse me, Raphael, but I'm going to call my friend again to see how she's doing." Debra stood up from the bench and walked a few steps before dialing the number. No answer, just a voice mail. She dialed the office number.

"Is Kimberly Montoya in the office? I'm a friend of hers."

"She went out of town for a few days, I'm told." replied the secretary.

"OK, thank you." Debra was surprised to hear that, since Kimberly hadn't mentioned anything the night before. She returned to sit on the bench.

She sat staring straight ahead.

"Did you reach your friend?" asked her companion.

"She went out of town. I wonder why she didn't tell me last night." replied Debra.

"If she was upset, she may have just decided to have a change of scenery."

"She was supposed to work with a client on Sunday. Kimberly told me she usually doesn't take off work. She's a top producer because she's a workaholic." Debra said.

"Workaholic? That is an American word I have never heard before." the Italian chuckled.

"Something is bothering me, Raphael."

"What is it, Debra? You looked worried."

"When Kimberly came to her seat just before the first act, I saw a red stain on the inside of her blouse. I was going to tell her at intermission, but forgot."

"What about the red stain? What do you think it was from?" asked Raphael.

"What if it was blood? Her arm could have been bleeding. I forgot to mention it last night. If it wasn't her blood, then..." Debra stopped at the thought.

"Debra, I want to ask you something. Do you think your friend knew the woman who was killed last night?"

"Earlier that night, we saw her boyfriend with another woman. I told her that I thought the woman worked at a local bank, but Kimberly said she didn't know her." Debra paused. "Like I told you before, I don't know Kimberly very well. We met through work. She's a top producer in town and I was flattered to be invited to the opera with her. I'll check the Sunday Santa Fe Journal in the morning. Maybe there will be a photo."

"Debra, I will be in town until Monday morning. Shall we meet again before I leave?" asked the Italian.

Debra smiled. "Yes. I would like that. I have to hold an Open House early in the day Sunday and can meet after."

"Open House?"

"Yes, I represent sellers who have their home on the market. Holding the house open to the public is a way to get more buyers over to see it." Debra explained.

"I understand. Shall we get an ice cream or gelato before you leave?"

"*Si, maestro.*" They got up from the bench and proceeded to the Ice Cream Shop on Washington Street.

CHAPTER 13

The second act of *Cosi Fan Tutte* had completed with a roar of laughter from the audience. The applause went on and on as each performer came to the front of the stage to take a bow. Then, the orchestra conductor took his bow and the curtains closed for the night.

Laura and Marc turned off the electronic translations in front of them. They looked at each other.

"That was entertaining, wasn't it?" asked Laura.

"Yes. I liked it more than I thought I would. It was light-hearted."

The air was much cooler now as they stood up to leave the open-air theater. Laura tightened the shawl around her shoulders.

The patrons lined up in the aisles to leave, commenting on the performance and the cooler temperature.

A Sheriff's Deputy and a Police Officer were standing outside the theater, observing people as they were leaving.

"Marc, do you think we should ask about the ticket I found earlier? Should we take it to the box office?"

"Let's stop at the bar a minute. I want to put it in a plastic bag to preserve any prints." They approached the bar and Marc talked to the waiter he had spoken to earlier in the evening. He was handed a plastic baggie.

Laura lifted the paper towel out of her purse and carefully deposited the ticket portion in the baggie. Marc sealed the baggie.

"Let's see if the manager is still there." Marc held his wife's hand as they pressed through the crowd.

Someone else was in the box office. "Excuse me, sir. I was here earlier talking to the manager." Marc showed his FBI badge.

"We're closed. I'm just cleaning up." the young man said. His ID badge read *Jerry*.

"Is there a way you can tell me who purchased this ticket? It's evidence we found tonight in the restroom where last night's murder took place." Marc pressed on while holding the baggie out for the man to see.

The young man looked at the ticket inside the plastic bag. "I don't know. I can try." He sat down at the computer and looked at ticket sales for the night before. He squinted at the ticket numbers and noticed one number was missing. He wrote the remaining numbers down on a sheet of paper and handed the baggie back to the agent.

"This is going to take me awhile to trace, since it's missing a number. Can I call you tomorrow after I've had some time to research it? I've got to get going, but I'll be back Sunday afternoon."

"OK, Jerry, I understand it's late. Will the manager be in tomorrow, too?" Marc asked.

"She's off on Sunday. I'll be in at two p.m. along with another person. I'll look into it, I promise."

"Here's my card. Call me when you have the information. I'll need the name and contact information of the purchaser, OK?" Marc handed him his card and put the evidence in his coat pocket. "Thanks, Jerry."

The couple followed the other patrons to their vehicles. It would be a slow exit into the night.

"Well, I'd say we did good tonight, agent." Laura said.

"We'll see if the prints on the ticket match either the victim or the suspect. I'll take the ticket to Chief Romero after breakfast in the morning. The Chief can fill me in on new details." Marc glanced at his wife "I'm glad we went tonight. We started the day not knowing what we wanted to do and ended up seeing an opera and investigating a crime."

"Yes, agent. On our way to La Cienega we go."

They merged onto the Highway then exited on St. Francis Drive. They drove through Santa Fe and over to Interstate 25 south. It was a clear night full of stars.

Marc rolled down his window slightly and inhaled the cool mountain air. Laura rolled down her window, too. "This drive is longer now that we live outside of Santa Fe. I hope you don't regret it." Laura said.

"No, I don't. We found a happy medium

for our careers and there's plenty of room for the dogs. We have a lovely home, Laura."

Marc turned on the radio to his favorite station. He was getting tired and needed to stay awake. He looked over at his wife. Her eyes were closed.

CHAPTER 14

Kimberly Montoya decided to stop at Ojo Hot Springs off Highway 285. She exited on Los Banos Drive. She would have a soak, then get lunch. She needed to unwind.

With the black sedan parked in the lot, she unloaded her duffel bag with bathing suit and towel.

She noticed a young couple strolling out of the hot springs entrance arm in arm. She was reminded of Andres. She missed him.

Kimberly checked into the Spa and changed clothes. She entered the warm pool of steaming mineral water. She closed her eyes and tried to forget about last night. She didn't like playing back the images, but it was like a scene in a movie that kept rewinding in her mind.

She had to think of a way to forget. She had to block it out. She would try to think of Andres as she last saw him. They had a nice dinner out. As they strolled around the Santa Fe Plaza, he stopped to look at wedding rings. He had talked about a friend's wedding that he attended.

Kimberly smiled. Maybe she and Andres would marry after all. This was a calming thought. She took a deep breath and exhaled slowly.

After half an hour, Kimberly toweled dry and wrapped her long brown hair under a baseball cap. She went inside for lunch.

The restaurant was crowded on this Saturday afternoon. After eating, she got an iced coffee and returned to her car.

She would take Highway 64 to Taos and stay at one of her favorite Spa Resorts on Kit Carson Road.

She turned on the car radio. A song was ending then the news began. *'The woman killed at the Santa Fe Opera Friday night was identified as Janice Blaine, a local bank employee. Police are looking for a person of interest. If you have any information, contact the Santa Fe Police.'*

Kimberly felt the pit in her stomach return again as she drove through the winding roads of the high desert. Who is this person of interest? Andres didn't see her at the opera. She had paid for her drinks in cash and Debra bought the opera tickets, Kimberly recounted.

She concentrated on driving the roads of the Sangre de Cristo Mountains and admiring the wide- open vistas. In another thirty minutes, she would be in Taos.

CHAPTER 15

It was Sunday morning in La Cienega and Marc Bennett was up at eight a.m. They arrived home from the opera at one thirty a.m. and Laura was still asleep. Marc let the dogs out in the expansive yard and threw a tennis ball around for them to chase. He needed to get limber so he stretched his muscles in the morning sun. Afterwards, he went inside and made a pot of coffee.

He decided to call the Police Station to see if Chief Romero would be in today. "It's

Agent Bennett. Will the Chief be in today? I have a piece of possible evidence from the opera crime scene."

"He's coming in at noon today." the desk sergeant replied.

"OK. Tell him I'll be in at twelve thirty."

After drinking two cups of strong coffee, Marc decided to go to the Village Store and get a paper. He jogged a mile into the village and smelled the aroma of fresh baked goods in the air. He bought the Sunday Santa Fe Journal and four pastries.

He walked home in a brisk pace and found Laura drinking a cup of coffee. "Good morning. I didn't want to wake you. Did you sleep well?"

"Very well. It was a long night. Thanks for letting the dogs out earlier so I could sleep in."

Marc took out the pastries and placed two on a plate. He handed Laura one. She savored the sweet apple filling in the turnover. "Oh, this does the trick." she said and sipped her coffee.

Marc opened the newspaper. He scanned the headlines. **_Murder Victim Identified_** *'The victim of the opera stabbing was Janice Blaine, an employee of a local bank in Santa Fe. Originally from Ohio, Miss Blaine moved to Santa Fe five years ago. She was newly engaged to be married. Police are looking for a person of interest. Contact the police if you have any information.'*

Marc looked at the photo of the woman. She did not look familiar to him. He showed Laura her photo. "Have you seen her in town before?"

Laura looked closely at the photo. "No, I haven't. She's very pretty. It's too bad her life was cut short."

"I'm going into town to meet with the Chief. I want to give him this partial ticket and see if he has any updates. Do you want to come with?" Marc asked.

"Oh, I don't know. I'll let you know in a few hours." she replied. "I'll see how I feel after I have some breakfast."

Laura sauntered into the kitchen while Marc sat in the living room reading the Sunday paper.

Within minutes, bacon was cooking and omelets were being made. "Would you like a western omelet or spinach omelet?" Laura asked.

"I'll have spinach. I like the way you make it with Feta cheese." Marc replied.

"Coming right up!"

Within ten minutes, Laura served the breakfast plates.

"This is good, Laura. Healthy and tasty, too."

"It's a good way to eat a lot of spinach at one time."

"I'll be leaving at noon, if you decide to come to town with me." Marc said as they ate.

When finished eating, Marc cleared the plates from the table and washed the dishes.

They watched the morning news on television and leisurely read the Santa Fe Journal. The local news gave the identity of the opera murder victim and showed her photo.

"So, this person of interest, does the Chief think she knew the victim?" Laura asked.

"He wasn't sure as of yesterday. He only knows the victim's fiancé was dating this woman at the same time he was dating the victim. The fiancé had yet to break it off with the other woman." Marc explained.

"So, the fiancé was a two-timer. You know the opera last night made fun of the temptation to be unfaithful, but it's really a serious matter. The opera was about women being unfaithful, but men are certainly to blame, as well. Now this fiancé was dating two women at the same time and proposed to one of them. What if the other woman saw them together at the opera?" Laura asked.

"We still don't know for sure if Miss Montoya was at the Opening Night. There's a BOLO out to question her."

CHAPTER 16

It was noon on this Sunday in July and Chief Romero came into his office with a glass of cold water. He buzzed his desk sergeant. "Call Mr. Andres Martinez. Tell him I want to speak to him again today, in-person."

"Yes, sir."

Chief Romero laid out the Sunday Santa Fe Journal on his desk. The murder victim's family had been contacted in Ohio and her name was released to the press, along with a photo provided by the bank where she worked.

He saw a new message from Coroner Garcia in his e-mail. "Victim's bracelet had three sets of prints. Get prints of the fiancé to compare."

There was a knock on the office door. It was Agent Bennett. "Hello, Chief."

"Hello, Agent Bennett. Come in. What do you have for me?" asked the Chief.

"I got the credit card number of Kimberly Montoya from the box office manager. You can cross check it to confirm it's the same person."

"Good work. Once we confirm it's her, we can track her."

"There's something else." Marc handed the baggie to the Chief. "Laura found this behind a stall in the same restroom as the crime. I thought you could have it checked for prints."

The Chief buzzed the sergeant again. "I need someone to check prints on a piece of evidence and I need a trace on a credit card."

"Yes, Chief."

Marc continued. "I have someone at the opera checking the ticket to see who purchased it. Since the ticket is missing a number, the man at the box office couldn't get it done last night. He's working on it today. It may be related to the crime. It may not."

"Laura assisted me in interviewing some of the staff. There's an usher, Louisa, who said a woman in a wide-brimmed hat came in late for the first act. The usher was about to close the door when the woman pulled it open. The usher said the nose and mouth in the photo looked similar, but she didn't see the woman's eyes. A waiter served drinks to a woman wearing a wide-brimmed hat. She seemed agitated about something. He didn't make eye contact with her, but said she had long brown hair and similar shaped mouth as in the photo." Marc explained.

"Laura asked the usher to show her where she escorted the woman to be seated and was told it was Row L, seats could be from 1-6. When I checked to see if Kimberly Montoya was on record for the purchase of any of those seats, they said she wasn't."

"OK. There's a chance someone else bought the tickets for her. When you talk to the office staff, ask about those seats. Who purchased those tickets? We can call those ticket buyers to see if they know Kimberly Montoya and if she was with them Friday night." explained the Chief.

"We need to get a DNA sample from Miss Montoya and her finger prints. She's not in our data base. There was a third set of prints on the victim's bracelet." The Chief continued. "Mr. Martinez, the fiancé, is coming in again today. I'm getting his prints. Maybe he has something with her DNA that we can use?"

"I'd like to meet with the fiancé, if you

don't mind." said Agent Bennett.

"No problem. Get yourself some coffee and a donut and I'll meet you back here in fifteen."

Agent Bennett freshened up and got some coffee. He skipped the donut today. He looked out the window from the second story building and scanned the clear blue sky.

He thought of the opera story from *Cosi Fan Tutte* and how it tried to make light of a serious issue. In real life, Marc knew that many major crimes had been committed due to intense jealousy and rage.

He finished his coffee and returned to the Chief's office. There was a man sitting in the chair across from the Chief.

"Agent Bennett, this is Andres Martinez, the victim's fiancé." Marc nodded his head and sat down next to the man.

"Agent Bennett wants to ask you some questions about Kimberly."

"We need to get something with

Kimberly's DNA or fingerprints on it. Do you have something in your possession that might be useful?" asked Agent Bennett.

Mr. Martinez thought a minute. "Well, I think I still have her toothbrush. I put it away so Janice wouldn't see it. I may have a comb she left at my house, too."

"Good. We need those items. We haven't been able to locate Kimberly. She told her office she was going out of town for a few days. Do you have any idea where she might go?" prodded the agent.

"Well, she likes to go to Spas around New Mexico. She doesn't take long vacations, since she works a lot, so she goes to resorts like the Ojo Hot Springs and the resort in Taos on Kit Carson Road. There's one near La Cienega, too. I think it's called Ojo of Santa Fe. I went with her a few times. She stays for one or two days at a time when she has a break at work." Andres explained.

"While you're here, Mr. Martinez, we

need to get your fingerprints. We need them to compare to those we found on Joyce's bracelet and on another piece of evidence we found."

"Am I a suspect?" asked Martinez.

"No, you are not. I will say your behavior with these women was morally offensive, but that in itself is not a crime. Since you knew these two women well, we need your cooperation in solving this crime." replied the Chief.

"I would like you to call Kimberly and see if she answers. We can put a trace on the call but you need to keep her on the line for at least sixty seconds, depending on the cell towers in the area. If she doesn't answer, leave a message. If she calls back, try to find out where she is." Chief Romero directed.

"Let's get your fingerprints, then you can try to call her." The Chief escorted the man to a room where an officer was ready to take his prints. Agent Bennett went to look for an empty desk to make some calls.

The Chief waited until the prints were taken. Then, the two men walked into another room with electronic equipment. Andres took out his cell phone. The officer behind the desk motioned that the phone trace was ready.

Andres dialed the number. It rang five times, then there was a voice. "Hello."

"Kimberly, it's Andres." He heard background noise, people talking and music.

"Andres, it's so good to hear from you. I missed you." the words were slurred.

"Where are you? I want to see you." said Andres.

"Oh, I want to see you, too. Hey, I can barely hear you." said the woman amid background noise.

"Kimberly, where are you?" asked Andres.

"Oh, let me call you back. I've got to go now. Bye!" replied the woman.

The Chief looked at the officer. "Did you get the trace?"

"No, it was too short. She's within about 100 miles in any direction. That's all I can tell you." replied the officer.

"Her voice sounded a little slurred. There was music in the background, so she was probably in a bar." said Andres.

The Chief looked at the clock. "It's one thirty on a Sunday afternoon. She's starting early. Ok, let's check these spa resorts and see who has a bar. Do you know, Mr. Martinez?"

"I know the one in Taos has one and the spa in La Cienega has one. I'm not sure about the Ojo Hot Springs." replied the fiancé.

"Mr. Martinez, if she calls you back, try to find out exactly where she is and what her plans are. In the meantime, an officer will follow you home to pick up Kimberly's toothbrush and comb. Don't touch the items with your bare hands. Use a paper towel and hand it to the officer to put in the evidence bag. You can go now." directed the Chief.

Andres Martinez left the police station and an officer followed him in his patrol car.

Marc needed to make some calls. He had found an empty desk and chair in the station hallway. He dialed the Opera box office. "This is Agent Bennett for Jerry." He was put on hold for a minute.

"This is Jerry. I traced the ticket you gave me to Andres Martinez. He purchased two tickets."

"OK, now I need you to see who purchased Opening Night tickets for Row L, seats one through six."

There was a long pause on the other end of the line. "There are three different purchasers of those seats. Marcus James, Letitia Hines and Debra Mason. They each purchased two tickets. Their phone numbers are....."

Agent Bennett took notes. "Thank you very much, Jerry." They ended the call. He proceeded to dial the phone numbers. He left two voice mail messages asking if they attended the opera Friday night with Kimberly Montoya. On the third call he heard a woman's voice.

"This is Debra. Can I help you?"

"Yes, Miss Mason, I'm calling to see if you attended the opera Friday evening with Kimberly Montoya?"

"Why do you ask?"

"I'm with the FBI and want to know if she attended the Opening Night performance. Did you go with her to the opera, Debra?" he pressed.

"Why, yes. Yes, I did. I purchased the tickets and we went together."

"How do you know Miss Montoya?" the agent asked.

"We're real estate brokers and met through our work. We're acquaintances. I don't know her very well."

"Miss Mason, do you know where I might find Kimberly? I was told she went out of town."

"I don't know. I was surprised to find that out yesterday when I called her office. She didn't say anything the night before about leaving town." Debra replied.

"If you hear from Miss Montoya, I want you to call this number. If you have any other information regarding your night at the opera Friday, please don't hesitate to call me."

"Yes, sir, I will." Debra said and ended the call. She sat down in her chair at the kitchen table. After returning from holding an Open House, she wanted to get off her feet.

The Santa Fe Journal newspaper was opened to a page she was reading. She looked closely at the photo of the woman who was murdered at the opera. She retraced the night, walking through the tailgate picnics. Her friend pointed out the couple. Later, as patrons entered the Opera House, she saw the couple again. The woman with Andres had curly blonde hair.

Both times, Debra saw the couple from a distance, but the woman in the photo looked familiar. It may have been the woman she saw with Andres. The woman at the bank.

Debra decided to call Raphael, since they had planned to meet Sunday for dinner. She dialed the hotel.

"Debra, how are you? How was your Open House?" asked her new Italian friend.

"I had visitors. One seemed very interested. If they want to come back, I'll know they are serious about it. Raphael, we discussed having dinner before you leave town Monday."

"*Si*, yes. I'd like to go to an Italian restaurant in town to compare to what is served in Italy. I heard of a place on Washington Street. Shall we meet at the hotel at five and walk over?"

"Yes, that sounds good. I will see you then." Debra ended the call.

She felt unnerved by the call she got from the FBI agent. She would discuss it with Raphael at dinner.

CHAPTER 17

A gent Bennett dialed the number of the security guard who worked on Opening Night.

"This is Bob Rios." answered the man on the other end.

"Mr. Rios, this is Agent Bennett with the FBI. I'm working with the Santa Fe Police Department regarding the opera murder Friday night. I was told you worked that night."

"Yes, I did. A waitress, Ms. Moreno, found me and showed me the location of the victim. Another guard called the police. I already spoke to the police about it."

"I'd like to hear it from you. What did you find when you entered the crime scene?"

"I could see the legs of a woman sprawled on the floor. There was a pool of blood forming near the wall. I tried to open the door, but it was locked from the inside. I told Ms. Moreno she could leave, then I radioed the other guard to get maintenance over with a ladder. I stayed by the restroom door to be sure no one else entered the area." explained Mr. Rios.

"How long was it after the first act had started that you found the body?" asked Marc.

"Not too long, maybe ten minutes. The staff often use the restrooms when the house doors are closed for the performance. I had to wait for the ladder to come before getting to the body, so that was about another ten minutes before I could open the door. Once the stall was open, I could see the victim was bleeding from her neck. She was slumped against the wall. I felt her wrist for a pulse, but there was none." said Mr. Rios.

"Was there any sign of a struggle in the restroom? Anything out of the ordinary?"

"Not that I could tell. When the paramedics arrived, I left the restroom and stood out front to prevent any staff from entering. The coroner came to examine the body and a detective worked the scene. I was told a murder weapon was found in the trash bin. Police taped off the area after the body was removed and the scene was processed for prints. That's all I know."

"Did you see any unusual behavior that night? Did anyone look like they were arguing or fighting?"

"No, Sir. The opera is usually a very festive occasion. Sometimes people have too much to drink and get rowdy at the bar, but nothing serious, nothing violent. This is very unusual. I've worked security at the opera for ten seasons and there has never been any trouble. I know the management is very upset. They have increased security and police presence now. We need to reassure the patrons." said the guard.

"Thank you for your time, Mr. Rios."

Agent Bennett dialed the Sheriff's office. "I'm working on the murder on Opening Night at the Santa Fe Opera. You had two deputies there covering the dignitaries. Did they see anyone suspicious entering the opera just before the first act? If they did, tell them to call me or Chief Romero at Santa Fe Police." Marc ended the call.

Agent Bennett went to the Chief's office. "Any news on fingerprints?"

"So far, we have three sets of prints on the victim's bracelet and on the ticket. Prints on the knife don't match what's in the data base. We need prints from Miss Montoya. The toothbrush and comb are being examined. We can't issue a warrant to search Miss Montoya's house until we find a match." explained the Chief. "In the meantime, we need to search the spas."

"I'll get Laura and we can go to the La Cienega Spa. If she's not there, maybe Laura and I can drive up to Taos in the morning." Marc suggested.

"OK, agent. Since it's Sunday, I'm short staffed, so whatever you can do to help in the search is fine with me. In the meantime, there's a BOLO out. If an officer finds her, I'll let you know." replied the Chief.

"Let me know if you get a match on her prints. How about the credit card trace?"

"It was traced to the same person at her known address. So far, it hasn't been used. She must be paying cash for her transactions." said Chief Romero.

"Maybe she's using another credit card. Text me with any updates, Chief."

Marc Bennett got into his vehicle and called his wife. "Laura, I'm on my way home. How about going to the spa in La

Cienega? Our person of interest is known to visit spas and I need to see if she's there. Are you up for it?"

"That sounds good to me. I'll pack us a bag with bathing suits and towels. See you soon."

Marc drove his vehicle south of Santa Fe on this warm Sunday afternoon. He was glad to be able to bring his wife along on some of his investigations. Laura was unassuming and observant of her surroundings. As an elementary school teacher, Laura offered observations that sometimes helped him solve crimes.

Marc arrived home after a twenty -minute drive from the station. The dogs wagged their tails as he entered the front door.

"Hey, guys." He stroked their foreheads.

He saw Laura. "Do you have a bag packed for me?"

"I have bathing suits, two towels, hygiene supplies, shampoo. Anything else?"

"That should do it for this visit. Are you ready?"

"Sure, let's go." Laura replied.

Marc filled Laura in on the case. "The fiancé called the suspect on the phone and it sounded like she was in a bar. He said she visits the spas. The police couldn't trace the call, so I thought we could check out this place. Her photo's on your phone. You can look for her in the women's locker area and I will visit the bar. I'll meet you at the hot springs."

They arrived at the Ojo of Santa Fe Spa and parked the car. Marc scanned the lot for a black Mercedes sedan. He didn't see it. Maybe she parked the car somewhere else.

They went inside and Marc paid the entry fees to the Spa. The couple parted.

Marc took his bag and walked over to the bar. He heard music playing and people were sitting at tables and along the bar. Marc tried to be discreet as he looked around. He decided to order a tonic and lime.

"When does the bar usually open?" he asked the bartender.

"We open at noon. People enjoy having a drink after sitting in the hot springs or getting a spa treatment. Sometimes, they decide to stay overnight if they get too relaxed, if you know what I mean." replied the bartender.

"Yes. I know what you mean. Do you have regular visitors here?" asked Marc.

"We have regulars. Some are professionals from Santa Fe who like to get away for a day or two. Some come up from Albuquerque."

"Well, my wife and I just moved to the area and wanted to check this place out." Marc said as he paid for his drink. "Thanks."

The suspect wasn't in the bar, so Marc proceeded to change into his bathing suit. He went to the hot springs. He saw Laura immersed in the warm water and joined her.

"Did you see her in the locker room?" he asked.

"No. I looked around and lingered as I watched women come and go. She wasn't there."

"She wasn't in the bar and her car wasn't in the parking lot." Marc let out a long sigh. "Well, we tried."

Laura let the warm waters flow around her and closed her eyes.

Marc enjoyed the soothing warmth of the mineral waters as he eyed the other people entering the water. If Kimberly Montoya wasn't here, he may have to drive to Taos in the morning.

After about thirty minutes, the couple exited the warm waters. They toweled off and went to their respective locker rooms to change clothes. They met in the restaurant.

"That was really relaxing." said Laura.

"I feel like a wet noodle."

"This place is so close to home, we can come here often. I can really use it after some of my assignments in the field." replied Marc.

They looked at a menu and ordered.

"Since you're still off work for the summer, do you want to go to Taos tomorrow? There's another place I need to check out." Marc suggested.

"Sure. Taos is another art community I like to visit. They have a museum of work by some of the famous members of the Toas Society of Artists." Laura replied.

"Good. I'll check in with Chief Romero in the morning to get an update. If this person hasn't been located, I'll tell him we're going up there."

They finished their meals and had another drink. Marc considered whether he would show the woman's photo to staff. "I'll be right back."

Marc decided to ask if the manager was

on duty. She was. He introduced himself and showed her the photo. "Have you seen this woman here recently?"

"Well, I've seen her before. She's a regular, but I haven't seen her this weekend." responded the manager.

Marc gave the woman his card. "If you see her, I need you to call this number."

"Is something wrong?"

"We need to ask her some questions. Thanks." He returned to the table where Laura was sitting.

"Any luck, agent?" asked Laura.

"She's a regular here, but didn't come this weekend. Miss Montoya must be up north."

CHAPTER 18

Debra met Raphael at his hotel this Sunday evening and they walked three blocks over to the Italian restaurant.

They looked in the windows of the many galleries and boutiques that lined the downtown streets.

"I like this town, Debra. It's quaint and very cultural. There is so much fine art and great music to enjoy. The hotel I'm staying at is top notch, as they say."

"Yes, this is a very artistic little city.

People relocate here from all over the world, you know."

"Really?" asked Raphael.

"Yes, I've had clients who moved here from other cities in the U.S. and from other countries. Sometimes, they buy a second home and sometimes they buy a permanent residence. Every so often, I need to hire a translator if I have a client who doesn't speak much English." Debra explained.

They walked into the restaurant and were seated along the wall. The room had framed photos of different parts of Italy.

Raphael commented. "There is a scene from Naples. Over there, is a scene from Florence. It is good to see these images. Now, let's see how good the food is!"

They ordered Scampi, Ravioli and Chianti wine. They feasted on garlic bread sticks as they waited for their plates to arrive.

"Debra, I told my friends about the

murder at the opera. They were shocked."

"Yes, I'm still shocked. By the way, I got a call today from an FBI agent. He traced my opera tickets. He asked if I went to the opera with Kimberly. I said that I did."

"Really, Debra? They called you? Something is very wrong, don't you think?" Raphael asked. The waiter brought their drinks.

"They asked if I knew where she was. The FBI agent told me to call him if I heard from her or knew of anything that might be important." Debra replied.

Raphael sipped his wine. "This is good vino." He paused then asked. "Debra, did you tell the agent about the red smear you saw on your friend's sleeve Friday night?"

"No, I didn't. I'm wondering if I should, though."

"Did you see a photo of the woman killed?" asked her Italian companion.

"Yes, I did." Their plates were delivered and placed in front of them.

"This looks *delizioso!*" exclaimed Raphael.

Debra decided to change the subject and enjoy the meal they were sharing. They clicked their glasses. "*Saluto!*" Raphael said and smiled at Debra.

They commented on the flavors of their meals and Raphael compared their meals to traditional food in Italy.

They finished eating. "You know, Debra, I would like to keep in touch with you, if that's all right. I have enjoyed getting to know you and your city of Santa Fe."

"I would like that. Maybe I'll take a course in Italian. I think it's a beautiful language."

They enjoyed a Gelato for dessert and Debra took out her wallet to pay. Her Italian companion insisted on paying the bill.

"Shall we take a stroll after dinner, Debra?"

"*Si.*" She smiled. Debra was glad to have

made a new friend this weekend. For now, she would enjoy their brief time together. She wanted to forget about the photo she saw in the morning paper.

CHAPTER 19

It was Monday morning in Taos. After spending a leisurely Sunday downtown and getting a call from Andres, Kimberly was feeling upbeat. Sunday afternoon she had drinks early then had a light dinner. She watched television and fell asleep early. She felt rested now.

Today, she would go to a favorite restaurant in town for breakfast. As she walked the narrow streets on Kit Carson Road, she reflected on the day before.

She had a feeling Andres would get

lonely and call her. She already had two martinis when he called. The room was loud with music and visitors, so she didn't talk long. She felt good knowing he missed her. She was glad she left Santa Fe for a few days.

She had parked her black sedan in the far corner of the resort's parking lot under a tree. She decided to take a precaution. She would take someone's license plate from their vehicle and put it over hers.

Kimberly had discreetly looked around the parking lot and noticed a car with out-of-state plates. No one was in sight. She took a wrench out of her sedan's tool box and unbolted the front plate of the other car. Then, she unbolted her plate and put the other one on top. If the police looked for her, they wouldn't match the license plates.

As she walked in the morning sun, Kimberly Montoya recalled looking at the photo of the deceased in the Sunday paper.

The woman had curly blonde hair and a nice smile, but was very plain looking. She tried to imagine what Andres saw in this woman. Kimberly felt she was much more attractive and made more money than a bank employee. She felt confident and glad that her rival was no longer in the picture.

Today was another day and she would just be a tourist in this high desert mountain town. Downtown Taos wouldn't be too crowded on a Monday.

The restaurant came into view. After the long walk from the resort, Kimberly was hungry. The place was crowded, as usual. She looked around and saw tables filled with visitors. She wished she had someone to talk to. Maybe she would call Andres later.

After breakfast, Kimberly paid the bill and decided to look for a Specialty Store. She needed a new knife. She always carried a knife or pepper spray with her and today she had neither.

She asked around and was told there was an Outdoors Shop a few blocks away. She found the store easily. Upon entering, she saw a glass case with an assortment of hunting knives and switchblades. A staff member assisted in showing her a few knives. She found one that was similar to the other one she had. It was easy to handle. She bought the knife and put it inside her purse. Kimberly proceeded to walk to the downtown Square. She found a bench in a quiet area and decided to call Andres.

"Kimberly, it's good to hear from you. Where are you?" Andres asked.

"Oh, I'm in one of our favorite places. Can you guess?"

"Are you up north in Taos? Are you staying at the Kit Carson Resort? I'd love to join you." Andres asked coyly.

"You guessed right, Andres. I stayed the weekend and will be heading back soon. I'll see you when I get home. I've missed you."

"I miss you, too. I'll see you when you get back." Andres completed the call then called Chief Romero.

"Chief Romero, I just spoke to Kimberly. She's been staying at the El Monte Resort in Taos. It's on Kit Carson Road. She said she's returning soon."

"OK, Mr. Martinez. I'll tell the Taos Police."

After ending the call with Andres, Kimberly received a text from the broker who covered for her over the weekend. "Buyers liked one of the homes. May submit an offer. FYI: Police searched your desk."

Kimberly's eyes opened wide. That means *she's* the person of interest. She rose from the bench and looked for a Hair Salon. She would have her hair cut. After years of having long hair, it was now time for a change.

She needed more cash and looked for

an ATM machine around the Square. She found one and took out five hundred dollars. She would get more later.

Kimberly found a Hair Salon inside the Hotel de Taos. As the stylist washed her hair, Kimberly thought of what she would do next. She had already switched license plates, so the police couldn't ID her car. Her name was on the Resort registry, however. She would have to retrieve her things and get her car. She would change her appearance before returning to the resort.

As she sat in front of the mirror, Kimberly watched over six inches of her long brown hair fall to the ground. She decided to get blonde highlights, too. The front desk staff wouldn't recognize her.

As she stared in the mirror, her head was buzzing. Then, she relaxed a bit, thinking police probably wouldn't look for her in this small tourist town.

CHAPTER 20

By early Monday morning, the Crime Lab had completed the report on prints and DNA from the opera murder crime scene. Santa Fe Police Chief Romero read the report.

Kimberly Montoya's prints on the comb matched the third set of prints on the ticket found in the restroom stall. DNA found on the toothbrush matched DNA found on the victim's bracelet. DNA was that of Kimberly Montoya of Santa Fe.

The Chief buzzed the desk of his

Sergeant. "Issue a criminal warrant for Kimberly Montoya. Search her home and office. Change the BOLO from *person of interest* to *murder suspect.*"

"Yes, sir."

Chief Romero dialed the Taos Police Department. "I need to talk to the Chief. Have him call me. I'll be sending out a BOLO on a woman who may be in your area. Her photo, along with license plate and VIN numbers will be posted. She's a murder suspect in a case here in Santa Fe."

The Chief's cell phone rang. "This is Agent Bennett. Any updates for me?"

"Yes. We've got a DNA and fingerprint match on Kimberly Montoya. I'm issuing a new BOLO. I'm waiting to hear from the Taos Police Chief. She must be in their area.

"I can take Laura and go to the Spa in Taos. We'll leave right away." said Agent Bennett.

"OK, good. I'll tell Taos Police you're coming and I'll tell FBI Agent-in-Charge Garland you're working the case again today. I'm getting a warrant issued and will have officers go to the home and office of Ms. Montoya. Be careful out there."

"I'll keep you posted, Chief." Agent Marc Bennett hung up the phone and went to the kitchen where his wife was cleaning up after breakfast.

"We're going to Taos, Laura. Let's pack an overnight bag and bathing suits, in case we stay over. We think the murder suspect is up there. There's a warrant out for her arrest."

"I need to make a call to have someone watch the pets. Then, I'll pack up."

Laura dialed a teacher from school who enjoyed Laura's dogs and had cats of her own. "Can you come over this afternoon? I'll leave a key for you. We may not be back until Tuesday afternoon. I'll let you know. Thanks so much!"

Laura fed her pets, wrote down instructions for her friend, then proceeded to pack an overnight bag.

Meanwhile, Marc checked his gear. He needed his weapon, ties, radio, phone, badge and cards. He decided to call the FBI office.

"Agent Garland, this is Agent Bennett. I'm working on a murder case with the Santa Fe and the Taos Police Departments. I'm heading north to Taos, where the suspect may be located."

"Yes, agent, Chief Romero called me. I'll need you here Tuesday afternoon. I have a new assignment for you."

"Yes, sir." Agent Bennett ended the call.

He heard Laura in the other room, talking to the pets. "Now, you all be good and watch the house while we're gone."

Marc appeared in the living room with his overnight bag. "Ready?"

"Yes, I'm ready."

Marc locked the door behind him and

they entered the black Jeep.

Marc drove to the Interstate. He took St. Francis Drive to Highway 285 going north. It was a clear summer day in July. They drove past the exit to Opera Drive.

"So, what does Chief Romero think happened?" Laura asked.

"It seems like an act of jealousy. Miss Montoya was at the opera and must have seen the couple together, though the fiancé didn't notice her. She must have attacked the victim within minutes before the start of the first act. She would have gotten into the theater just as doors were closing, based on what the usher said." Marc explained.

"How did she get a knife into the opera?" Laura wondered.

"I didn't notice any metal detectors at the opera entrance. She must have known that." Marc said.

"The opera may have to consider installing walk-through detectors after this." Laura replied.

As they drove, Laura scanned the vistas of northern New Mexico. "It's such a striking landscape and so desolate. It's no wonder artists are drawn to this place."

Traffic was light on this Monday morning and Marc took in the views as he drove.

"By the way, Agent Garland wants me in the office tomorrow afternoon. He has a new assignment for me."

"Oh, does he?" Laura responded. She heard Marc's phone ring. "Do you want me to answer that?"

"Yes, put it on speaker."

"This is Agent Bennett."

"Agent Bennett, this is Debra Mason. We spoke the other day. I went to the opera with Kimberly Montoya."

"Just a minute while I pull over." Marc saw a gas station at a nearby exit and decided to stop there. He wanted to concentrate on the call. Laura went inside to use the facilities and get snacks.

"Yes, Debra."

"You told me to call if I thought of anything else about Friday night. Well, I saw a red stain on the inside of Kimberly's blouse when she sat down for the first act. I was going to tell her later, but forgot. At the time, I thought that maybe she had inadvertently cut herself and didn't realize it." Debra recounted.

"OK, Debra. Thanks for telling me. Just so you know, Kimberly is now a murder suspect in the death of Janice Blaine. If you hear from her, find out her location. And Debra, be careful if you see her."

"Yes, I'll be careful. I'm so sorry to hear this. I saw the photograph of Miss Blaine in the newspaper. You know, we saw her and Andres Martinez together at the opera. Kimberly was shocked because she thought Andres was going to propose to her. She became very upset and was drinking heavily. When I called her the next day, she said she had a headache and hung up. I haven't spoken to her since."

"OK, Debra. I want you to call the Santa Fe Police Department and ask for Chief Romero. Tell him that you want to make a statement about your experience with Kimberly Montoya on Friday night. Tell him you spoke to me. Will you do that right away, Debra?"

"Yes, Agent Bennett. I'll call over there as soon as we hang up."

"OK, Debra." Marc ended the call.

Laura returned to the Jeep and gave Marc a bottle of cold water and a bag of cashews.

"Thanks, Laura." He took a long drink of water then got back on the road. "You know, I didn't even call the resort to make a reservation. Can you call while I drive?"

"Sure." Laura got her credit card out and did a search for the El Monte Resort on her phone. She dialed the number and made a reservation for a one-night stay. "We'd like to use the saltwater pool while we're there." She was told the warm pool was open from 9 a.m. to 9 p.m. She hung up the phone. "We're all set." She assured her husband.

Marc turned on the air conditioning. The temperature was in the mid-eighties. The direct sun heated the ground quickly at this elevation of nearly eight thousand feet. He considered what he would do when he arrived in Taos.

"We'll stop at the Taos Police Department first. Chief Romero told them we were coming." Marc noticed a text coming in on his phone.

"Laura, can you read me the text that just came in?"

Laura reached for Marc's phone. "Kimberly confirmed with Andres she's at the Taos resort. May return soon." Chief Romero.

"Laura, text this back. *I'll need back-up.*"

Laura sent the text.

Marc turned on the radio.

Laura munched on her snacks as she listened to music and enjoyed the views. She wondered what she would do if she encountered the suspect.

CHAPTER 21

Marc Bennett turned east on Highway 64, surrounded by the Sangre de Cristo Mountain Range. They would arrive in Taos in about thirty minutes.

"Is there something special you'd like to do in Taos while you're there, Laura?"

"Well, you know how much I love art so I'd like to visit the Harwood Museum. It features work by the Taos Society of Artists, a group of painters who formed in 1915. They came from different parts of the country and decided to stay and paint the people and the landscapes of the Southwest."

Laura continued. "When I worked at the now-closed gallery in Santa Fe, they had some paintings for sale by some of these Taos artists. Taos was a major art center in New Mexico before Santa Fe."

"Really?"

"How about you, Marc? Is there something you'd like to see while we're in Taos? That is, after you catch your murder suspect."

"Since you asked, I would like to see the Taos Pueblo. It's been continually inhabited for over a thousand years. The ancestors of the Red Willow People were living there before Columbus so-called *discovered* America."

"Well, it sounds like we have a plan. First, we stop at the Taos Police Department, then we check into the resort. If it's too early to check in, we can go into town.

Maybe we can go to the Pueblo together? I can get to the Harwood Museum on my own while you're working. How does that sound?" Laura asked.

"Perfect." He looked at his wife and smiled.

As they drove through the winding roads, Laura noticed some unusually shaped buildings in the desert landscape. "There's a geodesic dome out there." She pointed out of her window. "I've heard there are some earth buildings and domes up here in Taos."

"What's an earth building?"

"A building partially buried underground. It's supposed to keep the building cool in the summer and warm in the winter." Laura explained.

Pueblo style buildings came into view as they approached the city of Taos. Marc knew the Police Station was off Highway 64 so he looked on both sides of Main Street. "There it is."

The couple pulled into the Station parking lot. They got out and stretched their legs. When they entered the building, they looked for public restrooms. "Let's meet back here in the lobby." Marc said.

After freshening up, they entered the double doors that led to a receptionist sitting behind glass. "Can I help you?" asked the officer behind the desk.

Marc showed his FBI badge. "I'm Agent Marc Bennett and this is my wife, Laura Bennett. We're here to see your Police Chief."

"Just one minute. I'll tell him you're here." The officer got on the phone and made a call. She buzzed the door open. "You can come in."

Agent Bennett and Laura walked through the Station where officers and detectives sat at desks. Some were on the phone and some were looking at their computer screens. A voice called out. "Agent Bennett." A tall man waved them over to his office.

He held out his hand. "I'm Chief Mondragon. Come on in." They followed him into his office. They sat in the chairs facing the large desk.

"So, you think your murder suspect is in Taos. I had sent a patrol car to the hotel parking lots this weekend and no one saw a black Mercedes with the suspect's plates." the Chief began.

"Did the officer check the hotel registration for Kimberly Montoya?" asked Agent Bennett.

"No, they didn't. Since they didn't find the suspect's vehicle, they didn't ask if she was inside the hotel. What makes you think she's here, agent?"

"Chief, the murder victim's fiancé was dating the suspect at the same time. I just got word that Miss Montoya confessed to him that she's been staying at the Taos resort."

"All right. How do you want to proceed?"

asked Chief Mondragon.

"Laura and I will check into the El Monte Resort. I'll check with the manager to see the guest registration. Laura will visit the spa and scope that area out. It would help if you can send an undercover female officer over. Laura is a civilian, a school teacher. She's here to be an extra set of eyes. I don't want her in danger." Marc explained.

"OK, I'll call in a female officer. Since the suspect is female, she may go to areas where men aren't able to. I'll text you her name and give her your number. Do you mind if I take your photos to share with local police? I'll tell the officers you're working undercover up here and to assist if needed."

"No problem." Marc stood by the wall and the Chief took his photo. Laura came next and her photo was taken.

"Chief, there's a chance that the suspect knows we're looking for her. Her photo was sent out in a BOLO along with her DMV information. If she's clever, she may have changed her plates or try to change her appearance. When I get to the resort's parking lot, I'll look for a black Mercedes sedan. If I see any, I will text you the plate number and you can check it for vehicle registration. She may have, also, checked in under an assumed name and paid cash. I'll show her photo to the staff. If anyone confirms she's there, I'll call you to send in back-up."

"All right. We're here to help." The Chief stood up from his desk. The men shook hands.

Laura said good-bye and they exited the Station's desk area. When they got into the lobby, Marc stopped. "I'm calling Chief Romero quickly." He gave Laura the car keys.

"Chief, it's Agent Bennett. We got to Taos and we touched base with Police Chief Mondragon. He'll be sending an undercover female officer to assist. Has Debra Mason contacted you?"

"Yes. She said you told her to make a formal statement about what she witnessed with Kimberly Montoya. She's coming in this afternoon."

"Sir, she told me Kimberly had a red stain on the inside of her blouse when she got to her seat. When your officers do a search of her house, have them look for the blouse. It could have the victim's blood on it. They may find a wide brimmed hat and need to look for the engagement ring, too." said Agent Bennett.

"I just got the Search Warrant issued and two officers are on their way. I'll tell them what you said. Thanks."

"Yes, sir." Marc hung up the phone. He went to meet Laura in the Jeep.

CHAPTER 22

On this Monday morning, officers Corrina and Stephen were given a Criminal Search Warrant, which allowed them to enter the home of Kimberly Montoya. They saw the older couple on their front porch. The officers waved to the couple as they approached the front door. Officer Stephen had a special tool with him to break into the front door. They put on plastic gloves. Officer Corrina carried bags to collect evidence.

Corrina went to the bedroom and

bathroom areas first. She was told to look for a blouse with a red stain. She searched the laundry bin and didn't see the blouse. She looked in the bathroom and there were no clothes there. She found the laundry room. On top of the washing machine was a colored blouse. She lifted it up and looked at the sleeves. There was a long red stain on the inside of the right sleeve. The officer put the blouse in the evidence bag.

Officer Stephen opened furniture drawers in the living room. Some drawers had keys with address labels attached. Some drawers had fliers of homes for sale. The fliers had a photo of Kimberly Montoya as the Listing Agent. One wooden cabinet has various shelves inside. Officer Stephen opened the door. There were purses of different sizes. He looked for the fanciest one that might have been used to go to the opera. He noticed a smaller purse with pearl beads. His mother had one like it. She called it a clutch purse.

The officer opened the purse and saw a crumbled facial tissue with some pink smudges on it. He carefully took out the tissue and opened it on the table. There was a shiny object inside. It was a ring. There was blood on the ring. With his gloved hands, the officer carefully put the tissue and ring back in the purse. He put the purse in the evidence bag.

Officer Corrina came out holding an evidence bag. "I found the blouse with the blood stain."

"I found the ring wrapped in a bloody tissue. I think we can go now. Let's get these to the Crime Lab." replied Officer Stephen.

Near the foyer, Corrina noticed a wide brimmed hat hanging on a wall hook. She opened another evidence bag and inserted the hat.

They left the home and closed the front door behind them. Officer Stephen handed his bag to Officer Corrina. He took out a roll of yellow tape and attached it across the door. He walked around the back and placed the tape across the patio doors. *No entry.*

As the officers returned to their patrol car, they heard someone call over to them. "Is she OK, officer? Is Kimberly OK?" It was Marco Reyes, the neighbor. His wife, Rosa, stood next to him.

"Your neighbor is wanted for a serious crime, Mr. Reyes. If you see her, please call the Santa Fe Police." responded Officer Corrina.

The older couple held onto each other in disbelief. They slowly walked to their bench and sat down. Mrs. Reyes began to cry.

Back at the real estate office, another officer showed a Search Warrant to the secretary at the reception desk. It was to search the desk of Kimberly Montoya. The officer proceeded to open drawers and take out papers. He saw sets of keys with address labels on them. He saw a framed photo of the suspect with a handsome Latino man. The officer took the photo.

The managing broker was alerted and approached the officer. Other brokers looked on. "Officer, what is going on? Miss Montoya is one of our top producing brokers. She is well-respected in the community."

The officer presented the Search Warrant. "Miss Montoya is a murder suspect. I'm looking for any evidence that might be related to the crime scene. Now, if you don't mind, I'd like to continue my search."

The man stepped back in disbelief and returned to his office. The other brokers looked at him, then slowly returned to their work. They talked amongst themselves as their boss picked up the phone. He called an attorney who represented office matters.

"You'll have to re-assign all of her listings and contracts to another Designated

Broker in the office. Miss Montoya can still be paid her fee at closing, minus a referral fee to the agents covering for her. Remember, she can be paid only as long as her Real Estate license is active. Once her license is suspended, she doesn't get paid."

"I understand. Thank you." The managing broker put his head in his hands. He was not only going to lose business due to the scandal, he was losing one of his top salespersons. He stood up and looked outside at the blue New Mexico sky. He took in a deep breathe and got a fresh cup of coffee. He had a lot of calls to make.

CHAPTER 23

Marc and Laura arrived at El Monte Resort. Marc dropped Laura off at the entrance to register.

"I'll meet you in the lobby after I search the lot." Marc told her.

Marc proceeded to drive slowly around the parking lot. He was looking for a black Mercedes four-door sedan. There were two lots to go through. He spotted one and called the plate number in to the Taos Police. He waited a few minutes for a response. It was registered to a man from

Taos.

Marc drove through another lot. At the far end was another black Mercedes. Plates were from out of state. Marc called them in. He waited. In a few minutes, he was told there was an alert out on those plates. They were stolen. Marc kept his vehicle parked behind the sedan. He would wait until a patrol car arrived.

Agent Bennett decided to put on a pair of gloves and got a wrench from the back of his Jeep. He would remove the top license plate. He unbolted the plate only to find another one underneath. It was the New Mexico license plate of the murder suspect.

He put the stolen plate on his passenger seat and removed his gloves. He texted Laura. "Suspect's car is here. Be alert. I'm waiting in the lot."

He dialed Chief Romero. "The suspect's car is here in the El Monte Resort parking lot. She had a stolen plate over hers. I'm waiting for an undercover officer to meet us and for a patrol car to block her car."

"I'm calling Chief Mondragon. I want more back-up officers." the Chief ended the call.

Marc saw a patrol car arrive and he moved his vehicle so the officers could block the sedan.

"I took the stolen plate off." Marc handed the officer the plate. "This is the car of the murder suspect, Kimberly Montoya. Keep it blocked off until we find her." The officers nodded in agreement.

"Can one of you patrol the resort grounds? You have the suspect's photo, right?" Marc asked.

The officers nodded in agreement. The man on the passenger side got out. Marc introduced himself to Officer Ramon and they shook hands.

Marc parked his Jeep. He texted Chief Mondragon. "Where is the female undercover?"

The reply read, "Undercover is Jenny

Severs. Arriving shortly. She will text you when she arrives. She has your photos."

Marc took his overnight bag and went inside the front entrance. Laura sat in the lobby with her bag. "I've got our room key. It's just down the hall on the first floor."

"OK, let's go unpack." Marc waved at the front desk staff and walked down the hall to the hotel room. He was getting worried about Laura.

They emptied their overnight bags and Laura checked her purse. She wanted to be sure she had her pepper spray. It was still in a special compartment.

Marc checked his phone. He received a text message from Officer Severs. "I'm in the lobby."

Marc secured his weapon and ties under his vest. "The undercover officer is here."

"OK. What do you want me to do?" asked Laura.

"Let's go meet Officer Severs and we'll discuss the plan."

Marc and Laura returned to the lobby and saw a tall woman dressed in blue jeans and boots. She had a duffel bag with her. She stood when she saw the couple arrive. "Mr. Bennett?"

"Yes, that's me." Introductions were made.

Marc motioned for them all to sit in a far corner of the lobby, away from the front desk. He took the lead.

"Officer Severs, you and Laura can search the spa area. Show the attendants the suspect's photo. If she's there, call for back-up. Laura can text me if she sees her. Laura is not an officer, so I don't want her at risk. Officer Ramon is patrolling the grounds and another officer is parked behind the suspect's car in case she returns. I'll look for the manager on-duty and check registration for the suspect's room number and search it. Let's reconvene afterwards in the restaurant." Marc directed.

Officer Severs opened her duffel bag

and pulled out a shoulder-strapped purse. Inside the purse was her service weapon, ties and a radio. "I'll put my bag behind the registration desk for now. I didn't check in yet. Maybe I won't have to." She walked over to the counter, showed her badge and laid her bag down behind the counter. Laura followed. Together, the women went to the spa area.

Marc went to the front desk and asked for the manager. He showed his badge and was led down a hall of closed rooms. Manager Keith Davis was sitting behind his desk when he saw the men at the door. "Someone here to see you, Mr. Davis."

Marc flashed his badge and took out his phone. "I'm with the FBI. I'm working with Taos Police in search of a murder suspect. Her name is Kimberly Montoya. Her car is in the lot, so she must be registered here."

Marc showed the manager the photo on his screen. "Yes, I've seen her. She's been here before. Let me check registrations."

He quickly pulled up a list of names on his computer.

"Yes, she's here. She came on Saturday. Checking out today." he replied.

"I'll need you to let me into her room. If she's not in the room, you'll need to change the access code in case she returns." Marc directed.

Marc called Officer Ramon to come into the lobby. "I need you to assist as I enter the suspect's room."

Manager Davis took something out of his desk drawer, a Master Key. He stood and they walked to the Registration Counter.

Marc showed the front desk staff the suspect's photo. "If you see this woman, call police right away. You can text me at this number. She needs to be apprehended." Marc left them his card.

Officer Ramon entered the lobby. Mr. Davis led the two officers up to the second floor.

Meanwhile, Officer Severs and Laura

Bennett went to the spa reception desk. Officer Severs showed the attendants the photo of the suspect they were looking for. Laura wandered over to the saltwater pool. It looked warm and inviting. There were some women sitting in the pool, but none resembled the suspect. Laura went to look in the women's dressing room. Two women were chatting and neither one was the suspect.

Laura walked back over to the spa entrance and waited for the officer. Upon returning from the search, the officer said. "The attendants said the suspect has not been seen since last night. Let's meet Agent Bennett in the restaurant."

It was around noon and Laura was hungry. She would order a sandwich while waiting for Marc.

Officer Jenny Severs went to the bar and showed the bartender the photo. "Oh, yeh, I've seen her around. She likes to visit the bar. I haven't seen her today yet."

Officer Severs asked for the restaurant manager. A woman came out from the kitchen. The photo was shown. The manager nodded her head. "Yes, she's been here. I haven't seen her today though."

Laura texted Marc. "No sign of suspect here. I'm having lunch."

Meanwhile, Agent Bennett drew his weapon and carefully walked into the hotel room with Officer Ramon behind him. The agent called out. "Miss Montoya? Kimberly Montoya?" There was no response. "This is the police. We're coming in." The two men looked around the room. It was empty.

The men put their weapons away and Agent Bennett put on his rubber gloves. Officer Ramon stood by. The manager looked on from the doorway. "May I ask what crime this woman has committed, agent?"

"We believe she killed a woman in Santa Fe, a jealous rival. Can you get me a clean laundry bag for evidence, Mr. Davis?"

Mr. Davis stepped away for a few minutes and returned with a bag. He handed it to the agent. Marc noticed a journal sitting on the bedside table. Next to it was an opera brochure. The opera was *Cosi Fan Tutte*. He put both objects in the bag. He looked in the closets and in the drawers. He looked in the trash baskets and found a receipt to another hot spring location. He found nothing else of interest related to the crime scene.

"OK. I'm done here. Be sure you change the locks. If Miss Montoya returns, call this number." Marc handed him his card.

"Of course."

"Officer Ramon, can you patrol the grounds? If the suspect is not here, she may return soon. She's supposed to be checking out today." Agent Bennett said.

Marc put the evidence bag in his hotel room for safe-keeping. He proceeded to the restaurant where he found Laura and Officer Severs sitting at a table.

"No one has seen her yet today." said Officer Severs.

"I collected a couple of items from her room and her lock access is denied for entry. Her car is blocked, so she can't drive away. Officer, unless you want to order lunch, can you be on the look-out in the lobby?" Marc asked.

"Sure. I've already had lunch, so I'll leave you two alone now." The officer left.

"This really tastes good. What do you want to do now, agent?" Laura asked.

"First, I'm going to order a sandwich." He motioned for the waiter to come to the table and ordered. "We've got three officers here at the Resort waiting for the suspect to return. How about I take you to that museum you wanted to go to downtown?"

"Oh, great! It's on Ledoux Street, not far from here." Laura said excitedly.

"I'll leave you at your leisure. Just call or text if you want me to pick you up. Does that sound good?" asked Marc. His food came and he started eating.

"It sounds fine." Laura said as she sipped her tea. She looked forward to getting away from the drama at the resort.

CHAPTER 24

Kimberly Montoya looked different with her new hair style. It was much shorter than what she normally had. Her brown hair now had streaks of blonde highlights. She paid the stylist and left her a good tip.

With her sunglasses on, she almost didn't recognize herself. She decided to return to the resort, since check-out time was approaching. She just had to go to her room, pack a few things and pick up her car.

She left the downtown plaza and walked to Kit Carson Road. It was a sunny and warm day in the high desert. The hot sun was strong at mid-day. She wanted to cool off.

She walked to the side entrance of the El Monte Resort, avoiding the lobby. She passed a few visitors in the hall and took the stairs up to the second floor. Kimberly Montoya put her room key in the door. It didn't open. She tried it again. She turned the handle, but it wouldn't open.

Maybe they thought I checked out already? She asked herself. Simple enough. She would go to the front desk.

The woman took the stairs down and head towards the lobby. She saw a police officer in the lobby. She turned around and decided to go to her car. As Kimberly Montoya walked through the parking lot, she noticed a Taos Police car. It was parked behind her car. She was blocked!

Panic started to set in. That pit in her

stomach returned. She realized now that the police were searching for *her*. She couldn't go into the hotel and couldn't access her car. She decided to walk back to town.

She took the cap out of her purse and put it on. With this and her sunglasses, she would be hard to recognize.

Kimberly was getting hot and tired from walking in the hot sun. She had to go someplace cool. There was a museum nearby on Ledoux Street. Yes, she would go to an Art Museum.

CHAPTER 25

Marc finished eating his lunch and there was still no sign of the suspect. He and Laura left the restaurant and went to the lobby. He saw the manager behind the front desk and was called over. Laura waited in the lobby.

"Someone tried to enter the room. The suspect's room."

"When?" asked Agent Bennett.

"About five minutes ago."

Marc turned to talk to the two officers. "She came back. She tried to get into her room. Search the spa again. Radio the officer in the car to be on alert and look for the suspect. She would try to get to her car. I'm driving Laura to town and I'll be right back."

Marc took Laura's arm and they went to his vehicle. "I can walk to the museum, Marc."

"No, I'm taking you. Do you have your phone and pepper spray on you? Do you have money in case you want to buy something in town?"

"Yes, yes and yes." Laura replied.

"OK." Marc drove down Kit Carson Road to Ledoux Street. He kissed his wife goodbye and dropped her off at the Harwood Museum. He was glad to keep her away from potential police activity at the resort.

Laura entered the famous Art Museum and paid the entry fee. At the front of the museum were photographs of the early Taos artists in their studios. The large black and white photos showed the men in their work settings. Some of the studios were adorned with Indian pots and woven baskets.

The next section displayed works by Joseph Sharp and Bert Phillips. Portraits of Indian Chiefs in regalia and New Mexico landscapes were featured. In another room, Laura saw paintings by E. Irving Couse and Oscar Berninghaus. She admired Couse's portrait of an Indian Flute Player. She would check to see if there was a print of the image she could purchase.

Laura was so focused on the paintings that she didn't notice other visitors. Then, she saw a woman in a cap in the next room. Laura went to another area of the museum that featured modern landscapes by Kenneth Adams. She looked closely at a street scene in Taos. She didn't hear anyone enter the room.

"It's lovely, isn't it?" A woman's voice asked.

Laura turned around. "Yes, it is."

"I love the way he depicts the Taos landscapes. So much light and shadow." said the woman in the cap.

"Yes, like today. The strong sun creates shadows on the buildings." Laura replied while still looking at the painting.

There was a pause. Laura glanced at the woman and decided to go to the Gift Shop. "I'm going to look for a print to take home."

"Where's home?" the woman asked.

"Oh, outside of Santa Fe. How about you?"

"Santa Fe. I'm heading back soon. This is the end of my visit to Taos." the woman replied.

"Well, I hope you had a nice visit." Laura said and started leaving the room. She was feeling annoyed at the conversation. In Laura's experience, most people didn't talk to strangers at art museums.

The woman in the cap stayed behind and looked at the painting.

Laura felt uneasy. The woman looked

familiar. She had a suspicion. Laura entered the Gift Shop and took out her phone. She looked at the photo on the screen, then texted Marc. "I think suspect is here at art museum."

Laura took her pepper spray out of her purse and kept it in her pocket. She decided to look for a print by E. Irving Couse. The sales clerk took out two prints. Laura chose the Flute Player. As she was paying for her print, the woman in the cap walked in.

"Did you find what you were looking for?" asked the woman.

"Yes, I did. I'm so glad." Laura said, averting the woman's eyes. She tried to remain calm.

The woman pretended to look at books, then turned to follow Laura out of the museum.

"Hey, can I ask you something?"

Laura kept walking toward the museum doors.

"Can you give me a ride to Santa Fe? My car broke down and I don't know how I'm going to get back." the woman said. "I can pay you cash."

Laura opened the museum door to exit and the woman followed. The woman reached for Laura's arm. It was a strong grasp.

"Please, I need a ride." pleaded the woman.

"I didn't drive here. My husband drove and he's here working. We're not leaving yet. I'm sorry I can't help you." Laura looked closely at the woman. Though her hair was different, it was the murder suspect.

Laura's heart was racing at the realization. She stepped up her pace, but the woman followed her down the street. There was no one around. Laura put her hand on the pepper spray and took it out of her pocket.

Kimberly Montoya was feeling desperate. She needed a ride and the woman ahead of her wasn't helping. Her blood began to boil and rage was setting in, just like the other night. She took the knife out of her purse. "OK, sure, I understand." she said sarcastically as she followed Laura.

Laura walked faster to get to the end of the block where she might see someone to help. She saw lights flashing ahead. They were approaching, but would they get to her in time?

The woman in the cap raised her arm and lunged towards Laura with the knife.

Laura had caught sight of the woman in the corner of her eye and turned, aiming the pepper spray at the woman's face. She dropped her package on the ground as she tried to block the woman's knife from piercing her. She got cut and backed away from the angry woman.

Kimberly Montoya coughed as she held the knife in front of her, trying to get to Laura.

A patrol car pulled up in the middle of

the street. A black Jeep was behind it. Two officers ran over to restrain the woman, took the knife away and put handcuffs on her.

Marc ran over to Laura. "Are you all right? Are you hurt?"

"I have a gash on my arm." She looked at the blood oozing onto her blouse. Laura was starting to feel faint. She leaned against a light pole.

Marc pulled out a handkerchief from his vest and wrapped it around Laura's arm. "Wait here."

Agent Bennett approached the murder suspect. He took out his phone and held it next to the woman's face. Except for the hair, it was a match. "Kimberly Montoya, you're under arrest for the murder of Janice Blaine and for the assault of Laura Bennett. You have the right to remain silent. Anything you say can and will be used against you in a court of law. You have the right to an attorney. Book her, officer."

Marc turned towards Laura. He picked up the package from the ground. "I'm taking you to the hospital. You may need stitches." He opened the passenger door for his wife.

Laura sat down and closed her eyes. Marc put his hand on hers. "I'm sorry you had to go through that, Laura. We were looking for her at the resort."

"She wanted me to drive her back to Santa Fe. She said her car broke down. She got upset that I couldn't help her. Good thing I had my pepper spray. I could have ended up like Janice Blaine." Tears were rolling down her face as she recalled the attack. Laura started shaking and her arm was throbbing in pain.

"You're strong, Laura. You were prepared and you fought back. Give yourself credit." Marc said as he drove to the hospital ER entrance.

Marc escorted his wife into the

Emergency Room and registered her. "She was attacked with a knife and may need stitches." Marc showed his badge to the nurse. Another nurse came out and attended to Laura. "I'll be right back." He said and returned to his vehicle.

After parking the car, he called Chief Romero. "Chief, we caught Kimberly Montoya. She's being held at the Taos Police Department. You can talk to Chief Mondragon about the transport to Santa Fe. I have a few pieces of evidence from her hotel room."

"Good! Where did you find her?" asked the Chief.

"Actually, Laura found her. The suspect couldn't access her hotel room or her car, so she went to an art museum where Laura was visiting. The police and I were waiting at the resort. Laura recognized her and alerted me. The suspect demanded a ride home and when Laura didn't comply, she was attacked. Police arrived just in time and restrained the suspect. Laura's pepper spray worked to prevent a more serious injury. We're at the hospital now." Marc explained.

"Well, I'm glad Laura is OK, but that was a close call. I'll take over from here. I'll give an update to Agent Garland, too. You both take it easy now." The Chief ended the call.

Marc made another call to the El Monte Resort. "Mr. Davis, please. This is Agent Bennett."

"Yes, agent. The staff and guests are very nervous about this police activity. Any updates?"

"Yes. We caught her. My wife, Laura, recognized her and was attacked. We're at the hospital now. You can clear out the suspect's room and have her car towed to the Taos Police Station. Give her possessions to Taos Police. They will coordinate with the Santa Fe Police. Laura and I will be staying at the resort tonight.

To be honest, we're looking forward to a soaking in the saltwater pool." Marc said.

"This is good news. Listen, no charge for the spa services and free meals for your wife while she's here. I can't comp the FBI, but I can comp your wife for her assistance in catching this criminal. My staff and I are very grateful." explained Mr. Davis.

"I'll tell her." Marc ended the call and went inside. He took a seat in the Waiting Room. After about forty- five minutes, Laura came out. Her arm was bandaged. Marc greeted her and gave her a big hug.

"I got twenty stitches and some pain medication. It could have been worse." Laura said as they left the hospital. They drove back to the resort.

Upon entering the parking lot, they observed a tow truck hauling away a black Mercedes.

CHAPTER 26

After taking an afternoon nap, Laura felt more refreshed. The pain medicine was helping. She saw Marc sitting in a chair reading. "What time is it?" Laura asked.

"It's about five. You slept nearly two hours." Marc replied. "How are you feeling?"

"Like I had a bad dream. My arm is sore, but I feel all right. Now, I have a good story to tell the teachers when they ask what I did during summer break." Laura chuckled.

"There's some good news. The manager said you have complimentary spa services and meals while you're here. He's very grateful that you helped catch the murder suspect."

"Well, that's nice of him. Hmmm. What shall I do first?" Laura asked herself. "I think I'll have a massage. Then, I'd like to sit in the saltwater pool."

"Do you want to do that before or after we have dinner?" Marc asked.

"Let's do it before. I'll call the spa for the massage. Then, we can meet in the pool afterwards."

"Sounds good. I'll go work out in the gym then I'll meet you in the pool. I'll make a dinner reservation for seven."

Laura arranged for a massage in ten minutes. They put their bathing suits and toiletries in their duffel bags and proceeded to their destinations.

An hour later, Marc was sitting in the warm salty waters that swirled around him. His muscles were tired after a work-out and he was feeling relaxed now. He saw Laura approach in her bathing suit with a bandaged forearm.

"How was it?" he asked her.

"That was great!" She slowly descended into the flowing water next to her husband. Laura kept her bandaged arm along the rim, away from the water.

She looked at her husband. "Well, agent, we solved the crime of the betrayal at the opera. We don't have to check out until eleven a.m. What do you want to do with your free time?"

"I want to have a nice dinner tonight and turn in early. In the morning, I'd like to go into town and have *huevos rancheros* at a restaurant the locals told me about. Then, I'd like to visit Taos Pueblo. How about you?" he smiled.

"That sounds good to me."

When they returned to their hotel room to change clothes for dinner, Marc noticed that he had a voice mail message on his phone. It was from his FBI boss in Albuquerque.

"I heard that you caught the suspect in Taos. Sorry to hear your wife was injured. Take your time coming back on Tuesday. I assigned another agent to the case to start. I'll see you here first thing Wednesday morning. Prepare to be on assignment a few days."

Marc felt some relief that he didn't have to hurry back to work the next day. He would explore Taos with Laura. Maybe they would look for a work of art to take back home. He had a feeling she would like that.

ABOUT THE AUTHOR

Linda A. Morton is a former educator for the Santa Fe Public Schools and Art Tour Guide in Santa Fe. She, also, had a career as a Real Estate Broker in the Chicago area. After caring for her aging mother with dementia, she began writing novels. The author resides in northern Illinois where she tends her vegetable garden and native plants. She is a member of the New Mexico Book Association.